CHASING THE RAPTURE

MALCOLM ROSE

For Jess and Colin

With thanks to Robert Manning for legal advice

The brain disorders in this book are taken from real cases but the patients themselves are entirely fictional

Chasing the Rapture
by Malcolm Rose

Published by Raven Books
An imprint of Ransom Publishing Ltd.
Unit 7, Brocklands Farm, West Meon, Hampshire GU32 1JN, UK
www.ransom.co.uk

ISBN 978 178591 692 2
First published in 2019

A CIP catalogue record of this book is available from the British Library.

Part 1

CRIME

1

The guilt was clear on Martha's face. She couldn't hide what she'd done. The horrible smell of burnt silk was proof of her mistake. She held up her husband's shirt. The material that would have lain over his heart had gone. There was a hole where she had rested the iron for too long while she held her breath, distracted, watching the glinting knife in the man's hand closing in slowly on the unsuspecting woman. The woman was always powerless, always the victim, in TV crime. The gaping wound in the red shirt was shaped rather like a heart, near the third buttonhole down, blackened around the edge.

At once, Martha's concentration shifted from the drama on the screen to the coming drama in her own front room. She knew what would happen. She knew from experience that she would be punished. She was clumsy. Ben told her often enough. 'Clumsy bitch!' he always said. He shouted really. That's what ate away at her confidence. His constant heckling made her awkward and nervous. And she knew that this time it was his favourite shirt she'd ruined.

Ben stood up, staring first at his shirt and then at his wife. 'That's my … ' he bellowed.

She backed away. 'I know. I'm sorry.'

She still held up the shirt. Like a red rag to a bull.

He stepped towards her, picked up the iron from the pretty patterned cover. It was heavy and hot in his fist. Some black smoke rose from the charred fragments still stuck underneath.

Martha cowered. 'No. I didn't mean to. It was the programme … '

'My best,' he yelled at her. 'My only silk one.'

A small hand pushed the living-room door open just a few centimetres and a young, frightened face gazed through the crack.

Consumed by their own world, neither of the adults noticed.

Ben thrust the ironing board to one side and it clattered into the television. Now there was nothing between him and his wife, apart from the wrecked shirt.

'It was an accident. That's all.' Looking huge and bright, a supermoon shone down on the window behind her like a spotlight.

'How many accidents do I have to put up with?'

'I'm sorry. Really, Ben, I'm sorry.'

'This is the final straw.'

She dropped the evidence of her clumsiness and wrapped her arms protectively around her head. 'No!' she muttered pointlessly.

With anger and contempt written all over his face, Ben Clinkard raised the iron high. Then he let his frustration pour out.

2

Overflowing with lactic acid, her legs were like lead weights. Even her arms felt heavy and her lungs were on fire. She blew out the carbon dioxide and gasped down fresh air, fresh oxygen. Sophie's brain sent out an urgent message for yet more effort from her jaded legs. The response was slight: there was very little left. She was exhausted, gloriously exhausted. The only runners in front of her were a few men, twice her age. All of the other competitors were behind her as she neared the finishing arch with *Yorkshire Park 5km* written across the top. The clock showed 17:05.

There would be no sprint to the end, but her brain would not allow her pace to slacken. She would get a personal best. To the side, Mum and Dad were shouting, cheering like crazy. Her friend, Elizabeth, was jumping up and down. Her coach was scowling as always, concentrating on what could be better rather than celebrating the triumph of a PB. The crowd clapped and cheered.

Then, suddenly, it was all over. She crossed the line.

She stopped, bent over, hands on knees, and took great big heaving breaths. Sweat ran down her face and back. A voice thundered, 'Howzat, ladies and gentlemen! First female runner home – and first Junior: Sophie Lightwing. Fourteen years old.' An official handed her a bottle of water and she nodded her thanks. Someone else gave her a medal and a winner's T-shirt, and she smiled. Nothing formal, like a podium presentation of gold, silver and bronze, but in the park there was genuine appreciation of her performance.

Another runner pulled up next to her and, hands on hips, also took great mouthfuls of air. One of the stewards handed him some water too.

The amplified voice announced, 'Second Junior runner: Jonah Quinn. Fifteen years old.'

Panting, he glanced at Sophie and nodded. 'High-voltage run.'

Sophie took his comment as a compliment. 'Your name's Jonah?' With a pained grin, she added, 'You're a long way from home.'

The boy groaned. 'You're not about to crack a joke about living in Wales, are you?'

'Too good an opportunity to miss.'

He shook his head and drops of sweat trickled over

his cheeks. 'One: I've heard it seven hundred times so it's starting to lose its edge. Two: Jonah wasn't swallowed by a whale. It was a big fish.'

'How inconsiderate of him to ruin a good joke.'

'Good?' Jonah wiped his runny nose on his wrist band and finished his water in one swig.

Running a hand over her short dark hair, Sophie replied, 'The best I can do after a race.'

Jonah smiled at her. 'I need more water.'

He headed towards the table to get another drink. No one came to congratulate him.

Sophie had always run. She never walked to a friend's house; she ran. She never took the bus to the hospital; she pocketed the fare and ran instead. At school, she ran everywhere, despite the teachers' cries. It was what she was designed to do. Strong legs, big heart and lungs, thin as a rake.

Now, she relished her ability to leave almost everyone behind, to leave almost every*thing* behind.

'And then she said, "I don't want you out late. Do you know how many girls get mugged, murdered – or worse?"'

Sophie almost choked on her water. 'What's worse than being murdered?'

Most of the runners had scattered and the park had returned to normal. Elizabeth had returned to normal as well, complaining about her mother again. 'According to Mum, when they disappear off the streets. Abducted or something. Turned into sex slaves. Never to be seen again. She's paranoid.'

Sophie shrugged. 'Parents are.'

A gust of wind sent crispy brown leaves flying across the park like an aerial version of Poohsticks. As accompaniment, church bells began to boom chaotically on the other side of the city's green oasis.

Her mobile glued to her right hand, Elizabeth mimicked her mother's scratchy voice. '"Your skirt's too short." "Too much make-up."' She sighed. '"You haven't been out *enjoying* yourself, have you?" "Have you been drinking?" "Have you been with a boy?" "How old was he?" What a pain! Her purpose in life is to stop me having fun. I'll tell you what. She's scared I might have a better time than she did when she was my age.'

Sophie laughed. 'Probably.'

'I wish I could go and live with my dad and his new partner. She seems okay.'

A few metres in front of the bench where they were sitting, two blackbirds were flicking over dead leaves with their beaks, searching for grubs, insects and worms. Two hunched-up old people shuffled slowly past, with their faces set permanently to grumpy.

'Talking of being with a boy,' Elizabeth said, holding up the screen of her phone, 'I caught you at the end of the race.'

Sophie glanced at the photo. 'His name's Jonah.'

'A bit scrawny, but I've seen worse.'

'He wasn't chatting me up.'

Elizabeth nudged her friend. 'Yeah, right.'

Changing the subject, Sophie said, 'My knees ache.'

'I'm not surprised. You'll wear them out before you can walk into a pub – legally.'

Grinning, Sophie nodded towards two boys who were squaring up to each other near the café.

'Year Tens from school,' said Elizabeth.

'Yeah.'

'We could go over and stop them.'

Sophie shook her head. 'Let them sort it out like all boys do. They argue with their fists.' She seemed to relish the coming fight.

She didn't have to wait for long. One of them flew at the other like a wind turbine, arms whirling ineffectually. Slickly, the second boy sidestepped the torrent of arms and fists. He unleashed a punch to the side of his opponent's face, kneed him in the thigh, and it was all over.

Sophie said, 'Ah. I was wrong. They argue with their knees as well.'

The loser limped away on a dead leg.

Sophie rubbed her left thigh. 'Now he knows how I feel.'

'Actually,' Elizabeth said, 'he's not bad. Not the windmill guy, the short black hair.' Standing up, she smiled coyly at the victor. 'I ought to go and make sure he's all right.'

With a grin, Sophie shook her head. 'You're supposed to be impressed by brain, not brawn.'

'Nothing wrong with a bit of brawn – as long as it's got a pretty face. And it can make me laugh.'

'The other one made *me* laugh.'

'Yeah. For all the wrong reasons. Anyway,' Elizabeth added, 'you wouldn't be any good in a scrap at the moment. Not with your knackered knees.'

'I only fight with my brain,' Sophie said. She wasn't interested in boys. At least, not in the same way as her friend. 'Go on. Go and try your luck. Mum and Dad'll be waiting for me.'

3

The wind had died away, leaving a still autumn night, lagged by cloud, almost warm. Above her, the moon looked unusually large and fuzzy. Sophie was feeling good, her legs nearly back to normal. In the darkness she checked her phone and beamed with satisfaction. Joining an inanely grinning Elizabeth in a selfie was the black-haired boy. He's called Alistair, Elizabeth had texted.

Sophie replied, So you'll be out late. Try to behave. Then she turned off her phone. She pulled up her hood, slipped on her gloves, adjusted the haversack on her back and continued cheerfully along the street towards Elizabeth's house, knowing she wouldn't be interrupted anytime soon.

4

'When you've given birth, you have the luxury of knowing your child from point zero. Your right to be parents isn't questioned.' Mrs Lightwing continued. 'We didn't bring Sophie into the world. We had to earn the right to be her Mum and Dad. Particularly in her eyes. We worked at it the best we could.'

Ranji Nawaz smiled at them. 'Seems to me you did a good job.'

'We adopted her nearly four years ago – as you know,' Mr Lightwing said. 'Back then, she was adorable – partly because of her vulnerability, I suppose. There was something poignant about her being so lost, so damaged. But now – ever since the treatment – she's … '

Finishing her husband's sentence, Grace said, ' … a different girl. Joyful.'

'Yes,' Tony agreed. 'Such a contrast with before.

Talkative, kind, well-adjusted, great. And funny. She's *sharp.*'

Grace told the doctor, 'The other day, she said the girls in school don't work as hard as the boys. I asked her why not. "Because *we* get it right first time, " she said.'

Ranji smiled again. 'That *is* funny. From a female point of view.'

'I told you,' said Tony. 'She's happy as well.'

'You don't have any qualms about the procedure she's had?' Dr Nawaz asked. 'You haven't spotted any unwanted side-effects?'

They both shook their heads. 'No.'

'You talked it all through with Professor Dench?'

'Many times.'

'And you're pleased you gave your permission – and pleased with the outcome?'

'Very.'

Grace added, 'It doesn't take a medic to spot the improvement. Everyone can see it straightaway.'

'No odd memory effects that you've noticed?'

'No.'

'Good,' Dr Nawaz said. 'What about the future?'

'That's great as well,' Tony replied.

Grace filled in some detail. 'You'll probably agree she's not going to get a bucketful of brilliant GCSEs, but she's bright enough. And she *is* going to be an elite athlete. Everyone says so. She runs brilliantly.'

Ranji nodded. 'I've seen. She seems to run

everywhere. I encouraged her to jog along with one of my nurses. I don't know how best to describe it, but she looks awkward when she walks – as if her legs weren't built for going slow – but she's majestic when she runs. She flies. It's great to watch. Like a racehorse.'

'She's mad keen on police work and forensics as well,' her dad said, 'so there's a career if she wants it.'

For the last five years, most of Ranji's contact had been with her patient, Sophie, and not with her adoptive parents. She'd met them only twice. Even so, she knew a lot about them. She gazed at Mr Lightwing and said, 'You're a police officer.'

'Yes. I knew about the case against her biological father.'

'You could give her career advice. And a leg up, perhaps.'

'I can point her in the right direction, for sure.'

'Could you get her a spot of work experience?'

'I should be able to pull a few strings.'

Ranji nodded. 'Excellent. Is she eating well?'

'She is now,' Tony replied.

'She even gets nutritional advice,' Grace said. 'From her coach. For her running, you know.'

'No self-harming?'

'No!'

'Well, she's not my patient any more, but I feel … '

'She's not anyone's patient any more,' Tony pointed out. 'Professor Dench discharged her.'

'He's satisfied that she's cured,' Grace added.

Dr Nawaz said, 'Good. But I just wanted to say, if there's any behaviour – anything at all, anytime – that worries you … well, I'm always here and you've got my number.'

'You make it sound as if you're expecting … '

'No,' Ranji replied, butting in. 'Don't get me wrong. It's just that Professor Dench's method is experimental and promising, rather than tried and tested. It's still at the trial stage. Under those circumstances, I'm cautious, that's all. Watchful, if you like. If you bought a new kind of domestic robot to do the dusting, you'd probably watch it like a hawk when it got near your precious ornaments. I think you should keep your eye on Sophie. In fact, I know you will, because you have her best interests at heart. You love her. That's the best insurance of all.'

Sergeant Lightwing interrupted the chief's briefing. 'Hang on. Carmen Hope. Does she have a daughter called Elizabeth?'

'Yes.'

Tony sighed. 'That's … '

'What?'

'Awkward. I know her. Elizabeth Hope. At least, my daughter does. Sophie. They're school friends.'

'Do you know Carmen Hope?'

'No. Elizabeth's been to my house and Sophie's been

to hers – plenty of times. I've given them a lift now and again, but I've never bumped into the mother.'

'You're not compromised, then. No excuse. You're on the job. Inside knowledge and all that. Could be useful. But it looks straightforward. Forensics are already there.'

Tony Lightwing wasn't the best copper in the Force. His success rate was high because he was usually assigned to clear-cut cases. His promotion to Inspector was on perpetual hold.

'Okay. I just need to speak to Sophie first. Better she learns what's happened from me, not rumours at school. I'll call in on my way.'

'All right. Ten extra minutes aren't going to make any difference to Carmen Hope now.'

In a small office provided by the headteacher, Tony looked at his daughter and took a deep breath. 'I suppose you've noticed Elizabeth isn't in school today.'

Sophie sat up straight. 'What's happened?'

'I'm sorry, love, but … '

'Is she okay?'

'Yes. Elizabeth's fine as far as I know. It's her mother. I'm just on my way to their house – it burnt down last night. The kitchen exploded. Luckily, Elizabeth wasn't in.'

Sophie looked shocked. 'Is her mum hurt?'

Tony sighed and shook his head. 'That's what I came

to tell you. I don't know the details yet, but apparently she was in the kitchen when it … She didn't stand a chance.'

Sophie's mouth opened but no words spilled out.

Sergeant Lightwing reached across the table and took his daughter's hand. Again, he said, 'Sorry. I'll be able to tell you more later – after school.'

'Beth complained about her all the time, but … ' Sophie closed her eyes. 'She didn't deserve … '

5

The forensic officer pulled the mask away from her face. 'I can pretty much guarantee it was a gas explosion, followed by a fire,' she said to Sergeant Lightwing. 'The gas cooker was on and a neighbour's just reported smelling gas last night. Carmen Hope was in the kitchen at the time.'

'Suicide?' Tony suggested.

She shrugged. 'Unusual way of doing it. And she had a cracked skull, at the back.' She pointed to the spot on her own covered head.

'Someone clobbered her from behind, then?'

'Possibly. But all the window glass is outside – blown out by the explosion. No one smashed their way in. What's left of the doors and frames doesn't have any sign of forced entry.'

'No break-in. So, an inside job, someone known to

the victim, or … ' Sergeant Lightwing thought for a moment. 'Maybe she turned on the gas, tripped or had a heart attack or something, fell, smashed her head on the work surface and lay there unconscious until something in the kitchen came on automatically.'

'Like the gas boiler, over there?'

'Good call. It ignited the gas and … there you have it. An accident.'

'I don't think I'm going to be able to help you decide. There's so little left. Not even much of a body. The post-mortem's not going to tell you much. And establishing if there was blood on something within range of her head … well, the fire put paid to that.' She paused before adding, 'If someone did it on purpose, they did a good job.'

'You'll get fingerprints from the rooms that are more-or-less intact?'

'I'll make a list of everyone who's been in. I'll need prints and DNA from friends and relatives. To eliminate them.'

'I'll get onto it. We'll go door-to-door as well. Maybe a neighbour saw something and it'd be good to confirm the smell of gas.'

She nodded.

'I understand Carmen was separated from her husband,' said Tony. 'I'll check him out.'

The forensic scientist smiled slyly. 'If it's deliberate, you don't often have to look beyond the family.'

That evening, the Lightwings' attention shifted momentarily from fishcakes and rice to the local news on television. The item on Carmen Hope's death was brief and the police statement minimal. The report soon gave way to sports coverage and Tony tucked into his dinner again. He gazed across the table at his daughter. 'How did Elizabeth and her mum get on? You said Elizabeth complained a lot.'

Sophie glanced at her own mum before answering. 'They had a mother/daughter thing. More falling-out than normal, I guess. That's all.'

'Like what?'

Under the table, the black cat brushed repeatedly up against Sophie's legs. 'The usual things. Quarrels about boys, clothes, going out, and when to get back. Nothing serious. Nothing violent.'

'So, did they clash yesterday?'

Sophie nodded. Staring at her parents, lingering on her dad, she said, 'What is this? Why the questions? What really happened?'

'Probably a good old-fashioned accident. But … '

'What?'

'I just need to find out where Elizabeth was last night.'

'You don't think Beth … ?'

'No, I don't,' her dad replied. 'I just have to place everybody at the time the fire started.'

Sophie held up her phone. 'She was out with him. A boy called Alistair.'

'Can you forward that to my mobile?'

Sophie tapped the screen. 'Done.'

'Thanks.' Mr Lightwing's head sank down, then he pulled himself together and said, 'Sooner or later, Forensics will tell me there are traces of Sophie Lightwing at the scene.'

Sophie held up her arms. 'Innocent, your honour.'

'I know,' her dad replied, 'but you'll be on the list so – to avoid being accused of favouritism – I've got to ask, where were you at about nine o'clock last night?'

'You two were out. Not me. I was here. Doing last-gasp maths homework.'

Her mum's smile was crooked. 'Is that true, Sophie?'

Taken aback, Sophie said, 'What do you mean?'

'Homework – or were you watching telly or whatever?'

'How could you think … ?'

'Because maths isn't your top choice for Sunday-night entertainment. It's not your top choice for any other time either.'

Sophie laughed. 'All right. I change my plea. It's a fair cop. I admit it. I was playing on the PS4.'

'Are you okay?' Sophie held her phone tight to her ear.

Elizabeth's voice was shaking with emotion. 'I'm at Dad's.'

'You got your wish.'

'Yeah, but … I don't know. It's horrible.'

'Have they told you what happened?'

'Not really,' Elizabeth spluttered. 'Just a fire.'

'My dad's looking into it. He thinks it was an accident.'

'What else would it be?'

'Maybe she forgot she'd put the gas on, took a call, got distracted, whatever. Then it blew up and caught fire.'

'Why *my* mum? Why *my* house? I just can't take it in. I think, any minute now, she's going to come in and have a go at me for not being there with her.'

'I'm really sorry, Beth.'

'Got to go,' Elizabeth said through sobs. 'Dad's shouting for me.'

'Okay. I'll let you know if I find anything else out.'

'She'll still be dead. That won't change.'

'I'm sure you'll feel better once you're over the shock,' Sophie said. 'Take care now.'

6

'Are you stalking me, Jonah Quinn?'

'No.'

By the side of the track, Sophie checked her watch and wiped her brow. 'I'd never seen you before Sunday and now twice in a week.'

'I'm … er … a bit of a loner when it comes to running. But I liked it when we … you know … met at the end of the race.'

Sophie smiled. While she waited for the punchline, she tried to make him feel less awkward. 'Me too.'

'I hope you don't mind. I knew you came to this club because of the top you were wearing. I just thought I'd come along as a guest and see if … '

'Meaning you *are* stalking me.'

'No!'

'I'm joking. It's not a problem. See if what?'

'We might … be friends. I mean, we do share at least one interest.'

Sophie shrugged. 'Do you want to try and keep up with me for the next five laps?'

'Sure.'

Inside the sports hall, they both sat at a table in the corner and threw back great quantities of juice. Motivational music came out the speakers and inspired the athletes, particularly those heading for the track or the gym.

Raising her voice just enough, Sophie said, 'So, you're a loner, eh?'

'Yeah, I suppose.'

'Nothing wrong with that – if it's what you want.'

'Most of the time I like being on my own, but sometimes … '

'I've got friends who come and watch me. One best friend. Beth.'

Jonah shook his head.

He was clearly short of mates. 'Don't your mum and dad take an interest?' Sophie asked. 'They must support you – at least when it comes to competitions.'

Jonah smiled with infinite sadness. 'No. They don't approve.'

'Are they crazy? Why not?'

'They're both high-voltage doctors. That's what they

want *me* to be.' He snorted. 'I'm not interested. Not clever enough, either. I've only ever wanted to run. They don't see any value in it. They tell me I'm wasting my time. And my life.'

'Ridiculous. You ought to fight back.'

'Arguing makes it worse. I learnt that ages ago. Like chucking petrol on a fire. The only thing that makes me feel better is running – and that's what makes them hit the roof.'

'They're stupid.'

'All they care about is education.' He hesitated before adding, 'And girlfriends. They go on and on about the importance of thinking about a future family, but … well … not everybody's into … ' His voice trailed away.

'On Sunday, Beth thought you were chatting me up.'

'No. I wouldn't … '

Teasing him, Sophie said, 'Careful. You're getting close to an insult.'

'No. It's not that. Nothing like.'

Sophie smiled. 'Don't tell me. You're gay.'

Jonah shrugged. The gesture didn't mean that he didn't know. He knew perfectly well. Just that he normally kept quiet about it.

'Oh, you are. Sorry. Well, it's no big deal,' she said. 'Each to his – or her – own.'

With a look of relief, Jonah replied, 'You really don't care one way or the other, do you?'

'No.'

'You're only interested in my legs.'

She laughed. 'Your best bit by a distance.'

Shifting gear again, Jonah sighed. 'They're great for running away from people who don't share your attitude.'

Sophie looked more serious and nodded. 'I bet. But who … ?'

'My mum and dad for one.'

'They don't know?'

'They'd throw me out if they did.'

'They're mad.'

'Everything's black or white with them. You know? Right or wrong – and being gay is wrong.'

'Huh. I think I know who's right and who's wrong in this case.'

'We don't get along.'

'I'm not surprised.'

Jonah shook his head and then smiled limply. 'I've spent a lifetime not talking about this. Then you come along and, five minutes later, I'm blurting it all out.'

'Better out than in. Anyway, sometimes it's easier to talk to someone who's not so close.' Trying to lighten the conversation once more, Sophie changed the subject. 'It's not just your legs I'm interested in. There's your brain as well. The part that keeps you running when everything else tells you to stop because it hurts like crazy.'

Jonah looked into her face. 'Not just *my* brain. Yours

too. I'm interested in what you're running away from, Sophie.'

'Nothing,' she snapped. She stood up and strode away. After a few steps, though, she stopped and returned to the table. 'I'm just running. Okay?'

Jonah reddened. 'Okay.' Meekly, he added, 'I didn't mean to upset you.'

'I know. That's why I came back. And to say I'll be your girlfriend.'

'What?'

'If it takes the heat off you, you can tell your parents about me. You can even introduce me to them as your girlfriend if you like. We *are* going out with each other.'

'Sort of. Going out running.'

'The thing is, they might leave you alone for a bit if they think you're on the right road. The straight and narrow.'

Jonah gazed into her face. 'You'd do that for me? Really?'

'I like the way you run so, yes, I would.'

7

The young Sophie didn't have a memory disorder. Her memory was completely intact. That was the problem.

She could remember everything her father had done to her mother. The arguing. The slapping, the punching. Through the crack of an open door, the eight-year-old saw the hole in the silk shirt. Saw her dad's anger. Saw the heavy iron. Worst of all, she saw her mum's terrified face. Saw her dad's arm rise and fall six times. Saw red.

She had locked away every detail inside her.

Even though the nine-year-old Sophie didn't have a memory disorder, she visited the Institute for Memory Disorders, attached to the hospital. The institute had a good reputation for treating children and teens with post-traumatic stress disorder. It helped them to cope with disturbing memories.

The doctor said to her, 'My name's Ranji Nawaz and I believe you're called Sophie. Is that right?'

The lovable but mostly silent girl from the care home folded her arms on the table and then laid her forehead on them. Her long dark hair tumbled over her shoulders and sleeves. Her face hidden, she didn't answer.

'Do you know what my favourite animal is? Do you want to guess?' Ranji asked her.

The unexpected question got a reaction – Sophie's head moved a little – but did not draw a response.

'It's a giraffe. It's the huge long neck that does it for me. But there's a problem. Do you know what it is?' Dr Nawaz was certain that her new patient was listening, so she didn't change her tactics. 'Tomorrow's a creature comforts day. We bring in lots of animals. Dogs, big and small, a hamster, a lizard, I think, a tortoise, maybe a parrot. All sorts. But not my favourite. The ceiling's not high enough for a giraffe. That's the problem.'

Maybe there was a slight giggle.

'I quite like camels as well, but they spit too much. I don't want everyone to get soaked in spit.'

Another barely noticeable reaction.

'I want to make sure – if I can – that we've got an animal for you. So, what's your favourite?'

The girl muttered something but her words were trapped between the table top, her arms and her head.

'What was that, Sophie?'

This time her answer escaped. 'Cats are funny.'

'Cats. Yes. I think we can bring a cat in for the day. I'm glad you didn't say an elephant. That would be even harder than a giraffe. It'd never fit through the door. We'd have to knock a wall down,' Ranji said. 'Do you like those videos of cats doing daft things?'

The head nodded.

And that was it. Sophie went back into her shell, but Ranji was pleased. She had broken through. Tomorrow, she hoped a real live cat would encourage Sophie to open up, to begin the healing process.

It was a remarkable, touching moment. Smokey the cat put both its front paws on Sophie Clinkard's shoulders, as if it were sympathising with a broken human being. Smokey the cat allowed Sophie to interact with the real world again.

'A few years ago, when I was in training for this job, I saw something I shouldn't have. It was one of the patients doing something he shouldn't have done. I decided not to say anything. I thought keeping it to myself – keeping it secret – would be best. But … ' Dr Nawaz shook her head, 'I was wrong. It didn't work out. The patient suffered because I didn't bring it out into the open. Mistake.'

She sighed. 'I know better now. Secrets don't help.

When we see things that worry us, it's always good to talk to someone about it. Better out than in.'

Sophie didn't take the bait.

'I'll tell you what I do when I can't find the right words, Sophie. I draw.' She pushed a pad of paper and some crayons towards her traumatised patient. 'Maybe it'll help you as well. I'll leave you to think about it. But one thing I promise you. You'll feel better to get it out of your system and onto a piece of paper. You don't have to show it to me or anyone else afterwards. You can keep it if you want to, or you can throw it away. Ripping it to bits can be very satisfying.' She smiled. 'Whatever you want. It's up to you.'

Ranji left her young patient, but the hidden camera in the ceiling of her people laboratory recorded every distressing image that Sophie Clinkard drew. Her story came out in large splodges of black and red.

8

Posh house, posh people, posh accents. On the mantelpiece above the log burner, there was a large glass ornament in the shape of a lion. It caught Sophie's eye immediately. Very posh, very heavy.

Jonah's parents were dressed smartly in posh clothing. Mrs Quinn's hair and jewellery were immaculate. Mr Quinn's suit was sharp and his bizarre moustache was groomed to perfection. It curled upwards at both ends. Precisely symmetrical.

'So, you're the Sophie we've been hearing about.'

She nodded. 'Yes.'

Delighted that his son had a girlfriend, Jonah's father looked like a cat with the cream still dripping from its whiskers.

Sophie reached out and touched Jonah's hand, pretending she needed his reassurance. He nearly ruined the moment by jumping out of his skin. Just in time, he contained himself and played the game. He held her hand.

'We're very pleased to meet you,' Mrs Quinn said.

Reinforcing the message, Mr Quinn added, 'Indeed we are.'

For an instant, Sophie imagined he was about to add that they were beginning to suspect that Jonah was homosexual. She had come just in time. Disaster averted.

'Take a seat, Sophie. Jonah tells us you met on a run.'

The sofa was soft and plush. 'You're doctors,' Sophie said, plunging straight in, 'so you'll know that keeping fit is good for the brain as well as the body.'

'Indeed so,' Mr Quinn said. 'Activity wards off dementia in later life.'

'Hasn't some scientist proved that students learn better if they do lots of PE?'

'Yes, that's true.'

'I bet you're proud of Jonah's running, then. It'll help his education.'

'Not when he spends his entire time running.'

'In my school, the teachers make you sit down in lessons.'

Posh people's laughter wasn't real laughter. It was politc, political and patronising. 'Not *all* his time. That was an exaggeration. But too much time. It's a waste of any talent he might have.'

'Do I call you both Dr Quinn? That's confusing.'

Mrs Quinn's smile was skin-deep. 'Mr and Mrs is fine.'

Already, Sophie had figured out that Jonah's parents were warm and welcoming on the surface but glacial inside. They seemed emotionally disconnected from their son.

'What do your parents do?' the male version of Dr Quinn asked.

'Dad's a policeman and Mum … ' Her mother was into waste management, but Sophie didn't call it that. Making it sound nicer, cleaner and environmentally cool, she said, 'She's in the recycling business.'

'That's good, but it's not the safest occupation.'

'How do you mean?' Sophie asked.

'Soft tissue and heavy machinery don't go well together. We see the results of the accidents in A and E.'

'Oh, yes. One of them had half of his arm chomped off by a big machine. Gruesome.'

Mrs Quinn nodded. 'I heard about that case. Not a clean detachment. I think he's crowd-sourcing for a robotic arm now.'

'I confess we looked you up on the internet,' Mr Quinn said, changing the subject. 'The consensus is that you're a very promising athlete. A future Olympian, perhaps.'

'My coach doesn't encourage me to read that stuff, but I know what it says. In a couple of years I'm going to step up to ten kilometres and conquer the world.

Maybe. Maybe not. I just like running because I'm good at it.'

Mr Quinn agreed. 'I think you're right. At school, we usually like the subjects we're good at.'

Mrs Quinn said, 'What else do you like? Being an athlete is a very short career.'

Sophie shrugged. 'Science, I suppose, because I'm interested in forensics.'

'Very good,' they both agreed, as if she'd passed a test with flying colours.

Sophie paused before adding, 'You like blood in the body. I like it when it's splashed all over a crime scene.'

That posh, false laughter again. It made Mr Quinn's moustache quiver.

Sophie longed to jump up, seize that silly slice of facial hair between forefinger and thumb, and rip it off. It was like a spot crying out to be squeezed or a scab that had to be scratched. But she controlled herself.

She was aware that she too was a sham. She wasn't really Jonah's girlfriend. She was faking it – but she was enjoying it at the same time.

'But being young isn't just training for being old,' she said. 'It's when you have fun.'

'Explore and find yourself,' Jonah added.

'Yeah,' Sophie said. 'From what I've seen, adults don't have much fun, so we've got to do it all now.'

'It's true that age brings extra responsibilities,' Mr Quinn replied, 'but it doesn't preclude enjoyment.'

Mrs Quinn said, 'We don't think of ourselves as old anyway. Nobody does. Whatever age you are, getting old is something that happens in the future. Maybe when people get to their eighties, they'll admit they're old, but not before.'

'So, what do *you* do for fun?'

'We enjoy a game of Scrabble, a glass of wine, and a walk in the countryside.'

'Yeah. But what do you do for *fun*?' Sophie repeated.

That haughty 'ha ha' once more. Jonah didn't really deserve to have such snooty, obnoxious parents. Or maybe they didn't deserve Jonah.

'What do *you* do for fun?' said Mrs Quinn.

'Maths homework.' Sophie hesitated. She couldn't be sure that they recognised humour, so she added, 'Not really. I have loads of friends. You don't want to know what we get up to. And running, trying not to leave Jonah too far behind.'

His name seemed to act as a prompt. Jonah stood up. 'Well, it's time we … er … '

'Oh, yeah.' Trying not to appear relieved, Sophie also got to her feet.

'Time you what?' his father asked.

'We're going to a movie.'

Checking up on her son, Mrs Quinn said, 'Which one? A wholesome one, I trust.'

'Even the popcorn's full of fibre,' Sophie replied.

'It's a sci-fi horror thriller psychodrama sort of thing.'

'So much biology and alien DNA, it's virtually educational,' said Sophie.

'Yeah,' Jonah agreed.

'Well, behave yourselves.'

Outside, Sophie said, 'So that's what a job interview's like. At one point I nearly asked them how much I get paid for being your girlfriend.'

'I know. Sorry. You can't choose your parents, can you?'

'Well … ' Sophie wasn't ready yet to talk to Jonah about adoption. 'No, you can't.'

'Are yours any better?'

'You can come and see if you like – unless you're allergic to cats.'

'Have you got one?'

'Yes. They're … handy.'

'How do you mean?'

'You can put a cat among the pigeons, let one out of the bag, or swing one in a small room.' She laughed. 'Joke. Yes, we've got one. Pudding. She likes rubbing up against runners' legs. Anyway, we're not really going to see a film, are we?'

'Not that I know about.'

'You'd better look up what's on – in case they quiz you when you get back.' She looked at him and said, 'You know, one day, you'll have to take a boyfriend home and say, "Yes, I'm gay. Just get over it."'

'That's the day they'll kill me.'

'Well, you can't keep it secret till they die. They look pretty fit for their age.'

Jonah shrugged helplessly.

Sophie smiled. 'You'll have to pick a boyfriend with a bit of beef. A bodyguard or a bouncer for protection. Even better, date a multiple murderer.'

9

'Boyfriend?' her mum said with a smile.

'In the sense that he's a friend who's a boy.'

Sophie's dad shook Jonah's hand warmly. 'Haven't I seen you somewhere before?'

In a flash, Sophie said, 'Wanted poster. Mass murder.'

'I think it was the Yorkshire Park race,' Jonah replied. 'Sophie beat me. Not by much, though.'

'Ah, yes. I remember. You did well.'

'Thanks.'

Pudding came in through the cat flap, took one look at the unexpected gathering in the hall, and dropped a lame mouse on the carpet. It was barely alive.

'Talking of mass murderers … ' said Sophie.

'I'll deal with it,' Mr Lightwing sighed.

Sophie nodded. 'Kill it quickly. The mouse, I mean.'

Her dad let out a weary breath. 'I wasn't going to torture it first. Not like Pudding.'

'Why's he – she – called Pudding?' Jonah asked.

'She's black. Black Pudding.'

'By that logic, you could have called her Bird or Mail,' said Jonah.

'Or Death,' her father added as he grasped the mouse's tail between his fingers and lifted up the helpless creature. It didn't even struggle.

'Or Sheep. Or Widow,' said Sophie.

'Or Coffee. Which reminds me. Who's having tea, coffee or whatever?' Grace asked.

'Whatever would be good,' Sophie replied. 'If it's in a can and full of sugar.'

The atmosphere was completely different in the Lightwings' house. Like four friends sitting down together, having a drink and a chat. Certainly not like an interview.

'Any news on Beth's mum?' Sophie asked her dad.

Sergeant Lightwing glanced at Jonah, clearly not wanting to open up in front of a stranger. 'Not really,' he replied. 'But everything still points to an accident.'

'Did they find my fingerprints?'

'Yes. But nowhere incriminating,' he said with a smile. 'And no motive. So you're in the clear.'

'You wouldn't have been able to arrest me anyway,' she replied. 'I'd be too fast for you.'

'That's true.' The policeman turned towards Jonah. 'Are you in a running club?'

'I wasn't,' he answered, 'but it looks like I'm joining Sophie's.'

Mr Lightwing nodded. 'That's good. You can encourage each other.'

'I'm a year older than her – and I'm a boy – but trying to keep up with her is a bit scary,' said Jonah.

Sophie smiled. 'I knew a boy who was scared of buttons.'

'Buttons?' Jonah exclaimed.

'Yeah. I thought it was a joke as well. But it wasn't. It was hell for him. Owen, he was called. If he saw a button, it was like drowning, he said. He couldn't breathe.'

'Why?'

Sophie shrugged. 'I dunno. Why are loads of people scared of spiders?'

'Because some are poisonous.'

'Not in this country, they're not. Anyway, this button thing isn't as unusual as you think. It's even got a name. Koumpounophobia. Or something like that.'

Sophie's parents looked surprised at the turn in the conversation, but they both nodded. Plainly, they knew what she was talking about.

'But buttons are everywhere,' said Jonah.

'Exactly. Shirts, blouses, jackets. He couldn't go to school. Couldn't bear to see anyone in a uniform, couldn't wear the uniform. Only T-shirts, sweat shirts and that sort of thing. It pretty much ruined his life.'

'Weird.'

'He's fixed now.'

'There's a cure?'

Mr and Mrs Lightwing held their breaths, not sure how far Sophie would go.

'Yes,' she said. 'They can tweak your brain for that sort of thing.'

10

Sophie Clinkard showed the classic symptoms of post-traumatic stress disorder: fear, sadness, aggression, nightmares and isolation. She also self-harmed. There were six ugly notches on her left arm. She didn't suffer flashbacks of what she'd seen in her family's living room, but she repeated part of the trauma perpetually in play. Her only game was pretend-ironing and it always ended with her venting her anger on the clothes. She screwed them up and ripped them if she could. If she'd been near a source of heat, no doubt she would have burnt them.

Every trick in the manual for treating children with PTSD had bounced off Sophie without leaving a mark. No beneficial effect at all.

Play therapy should have helped her to manage her painful memories, but it left her even more distressed.

Ranji Nawaz tried trauma-focused cognitive behavioural therapy. One small step at a time, Ranji hoped to help Sophie develop a strategy for coping. She hoped to teach the girl to become her own therapist.

At a table in the Institute for Memory Disorders, Ranji asked her young, damaged patient, 'How do you feel about going into a living room?'

Sophie mumbled, 'Bad. I don't like it.'

'So, what do you do?'

'I don't go in. If I have to, I run in and straight out.'

'What are you thinking that makes you do that?'

'It's like the room where Mum died.'

The therapist nodded. 'That's bound to make you feel bad.'

'Yes.'

'And that feeling's what makes you run away?'

'Yes.'

Dr Nawaz drew a large triangle on a piece of paper and began to write labels on it. 'This side's for thoughts,' she said. 'This one here is for feelings and the third one's for behaviour. Because that's how it works, isn't it? We think about something. The thought makes us feel happy, or sad or whatever. And that affects what we do. What we're feeling makes us behave in a certain way.'

Sophie had seen the triangle before. She didn't respond.

On the thought side of the triangle, Ranji wrote with a blue pen: *Mum and Dad arguing*. On the feelings side, she simply jotted: *Bad.* On the third side, she summarised Sophie's reaction as: *Run out.*

'Is there anything else that happened in your living room back home?' Ranji asked. 'Something nice?'

'I had birthday parties, I suppose. We watched TV, played games sometimes. And that's where the Christmas tree went.' Sophie shrugged.

'Great. How do you feel when you think about parties?'

'Good.'

'Yeah. Parties *are* good. Happy.'

'We had a clown once. He was funny.'

'Did he fall over?'

'Yes. He did magic, but it all went wrong.'

'That *is* funny.' But Ranji did not dwell on the clown. For some patients, clowns could become sinister. Instead, she asked, 'Did you get presents, Sophie?'

'Yes.'

'Do you like getting presents?'

'Yes.'

'How does it make you feel?'

'Happy. Makes me think people must like me.'

'Good point. They must, mustn't they? To give you presents.'

'Yes.'

'So, if you go into a living room, could you think about a birthday party and presents? Would that change what you did? You wouldn't have to rush out?'

'Maybe.'

'You see, you don't have to think about the sad thing. It happened and you'll think about it sometimes, for sure, but it doesn't have to be on your mind all the time. I want you to think about happy things as well. Will you do that for me? I'd love it if you went into a living room and thought about people liking you so much they give you presents on your birthday. Yes?'

'Yes.'

'It'll take a bit of practice. Think good thoughts. Birthday and Christmas presents.' Using a bright green pen, she wrote *Birthday party* and *presents* near the top of the right-hand side of the triangle, *Happy* in the middle of the bottom, and *Sit down – no running out* on the left-hand side.

'All right.'

'That'd be great, Sophie.'

Sophie tried. She really did. She sat down in a living room – and all the time rubbed her hand heavily over the edge of the chair until she had scraped away the skin.

Sophie's school had called the Institute for Memory Disorders to warn Dr Nawaz that a member of staff was on her way with Sophie Clinkard. She'd had a complete meltdown in one of the lessons and the school could no longer cope with her.

Once Ranji had calmed Sophie down – going through a process of deep breathing relaxation – she said, 'I heard you didn't have a good day at school today.'

'No.'

'It was in a science lesson, wasn't it? What happened?'

'I don't like the teacher.'

'Why not?'

'He's a man and he came over to me.'

Ranji thought for a moment. 'Was he holding anything?'

'A rock. He said it was a fossil.'

Ranji nodded. It was clear to her that Sophie had braced herself for an attack. She'd expected him to let fly at her with the stone – like her father once let fly with an iron – so she had flipped.

Ranji smiled at her. 'I'm sure he was trying to show you something he thought you'd like to see. Something interesting. That's all.'

'I don't like him.'

Ranji shuffled closer to her patient. Sophie would never be able to live a normal life if she carried on believing that all men hit women. The time had come to challenge her misconception.

'When something bad happens,' Ranji said, 'a lot of people try to avoid thinking about it – and don't talk about it – because it's upsetting. But bottling it up like this keeps you on edge all the time and stops you making sense of what's happened. Then your brain can't pack it safely away.'

Sophie sat and listened – probably – but she didn't react. She wound her hair tightly round the fingers of her right hand.

'You don't have to be afraid of a memory, Sophie. A memory is just a thought. Thinking about it won't make it happen again. You're safe. A memory can make you *feel* bad, though. It can make you act in a particular way, but it can't actually hurt you. On top of that, *you* can change the way it makes you feel. That's what this is all about. Helping you to think differently.'

Still Sophie kept quiet, tugging at her hair.

'We can't turn back time and stop what happened to your mum. Sadly. We have to deal with it in the here and now. So, I want you to talk me through that night. Tell me what happened. And, while you do it, I'd like to know your hotspots. In other words, I want you to tell me when your feelings are strongest. Use this scale.' Ranji pointed to a thermometer shape on a piece of paper. 'One to ten. One, you hardly feel a thing. Ten, it makes you feel really, really emotional. Is that all right? Can you do that? You can stop and relax at any time. Remember the deep breathing I showed you.'

'Okay.'

'You're in safe hands. It's just you and me.' Ranji smiled and touched her patient's left hand where it rested on the thermometer in the region of two/three. 'Let's start, shall we? Take your time. You heard some shouting. Your mum and dad. You went to investigate. Tell me what you saw, heard, smelled. Anything.'

'They fought lots but … I don't know … this time it was different. There was a great big moon. It lit the stairs up. And there was a horrid smell.' At once, her fingers slid up the anxiety scale from three to seven.

Smells were powerful reminders, so Ranji wasn't surprised that the mercury was rising fast as her patient recalled the stench of the smouldering shirt. She decided not to intervene. Yet.

'I pushed the door open, just a bit. It was the usual. Dad was shouting at Mum.' Her hand came back down the scale a little. Rows were not uncommon. Sophie was accustomed to them. She took five deep breaths. 'Mum was holding a shirt. There was a film on telly, I think. Dad smashed it. He'd got the iron. It was smoking.'

Inevitably Sophie's fingers rose back up the thermometer.

'Mum sort of fell back. Dad held up the iron and then bashed it down, pointy end first.' Her hand reached the top of the anxiety scale. 'Six times, he did it. I counted. I couldn't see properly. But … '

'Relax. Deep breaths. Then tell me.'

'It was a big splash of red. Like a fountain. I didn't want to … But I knew what it was. I ran upstairs.'

'What did you do?'

'Nothing. I hid under the blanket. I was scared.'

'Did your dad come up to see you?'

'No.'

Ranji nodded. 'Did you go to sleep?'

'No. Mum used to sing me a song when I couldn't get to sleep. I knew she wouldn't do that any more.'

'Who do you blame for what happened, Sophie?'

Her hand remained fixed to the top of the thermometer. 'I don't know. Maybe if I'd … '

Ranji shook her head. 'No, Sophie, not you. It was nothing to do with you. It was all about your mum, your dad and a shirt. There was nothing you could have done to change things.' Again, Ranji touched Sophie's arm. 'It won't happen again. He's in prison for what he did. And you have to remember this. Not all men are like your father. I've been married a long time and my husband hasn't got close to raising his hand – against me or anyone else. Even when he's mad about something. It wouldn't enter his head to take it out on another person. And I'm sure your teacher's the same.'

Sophie did not seem reassured.

'I don't know exactly what was on your dad's mind that night, but he didn't do it to hurt you. He loved you. He probably loved your mum as well – in his own way. What happened was, he lost his temper. In that moment, he wanted to hurt the person who'd made a mistake. Not you. Your dad's triangle was something like this. Thought: my wife's ruined my best shirt. Feelings: angry and frustrated. Behaviour: hit out at her.' Ranji paused and smiled sadly at her patient. 'I bet your mum and dad shared some good times as well.'

In effect, the session was over. Ranji continued to talk, trying to identify unhelpful thoughts and to replace them with something more proactive and positive, to help Sophie make sense of what had happened, to reassure her that nightmares and fear were common reactions to trauma, but Sophie had switched off altogether.

Talking therapy was going the same way as play therapy.

The air was thick with the sulphurous stench of fireworks and smoke. Sophie sat on the floor in the corner of the room, arms wrapped protectively over her head, whimpering like a family pet scared of the bangs and flashes of bonfire night.

January. A new year. The day was clear and sharp, the sky blue. Frost covered each blade of grass with white whiskers. Roads and pavements glistened with silvery stubble and every puddle had a thick crusty coating of ice. Like everyone else's, Sophie's breath came out as a mini-cloud.

She was doing fine until, behind her, a boy pressed his shoe innocently on a frozen puddle and the pressure cracked the layer of ice. The sound sent Sophie into an immediate panic attack and she let out a long series of piercing squeals.

'I heard a noise,' she explained to Ranji later. 'It was like ... cracking an egg, only loud. Very loud. Horrid.'

Ranji nodded. No doubt, it was just like the sound of a skull cracking.

January. A new year. A new crisis.

'In my view,' Dr Nawaz said into her phone, 'you should go for adoption as soon as possible. Sophie needs to be in a stable, loving family. But you'll have to vet would-be parents very carefully indeed. In particular, the father's got to be the right man for the job. That's the most important thing.' Knowing that she had to be specific and firm with Social Services, Ranji added, 'He's got to be well-grounded, a community man, loving, respected, free of even the slightest whiff of domestic abuse. And the understanding sort. He's got to cope with childhood challenges on a massive scale and never ever lose his cool. The mother needs to sing a lullaby each night. This might sound like a tiny thing to you and me but it's enormous for Sophie. And no burning smells. This family can't have a log fire or anything similar. The smell would make Sophie implode at this stage. And any ironing needs to be done while she's asleep. At least at first. I'll email you my notes so you can work around all the issues. And any possible family will have to see them as well – so they know what they're taking on.'

'Sounds like this placement's going to take an age – to get the right people and the right environment.'

'The sooner you start the process, the sooner she'll get the stability she needs.'

Sophie bunked off school a lot so she could run. Run hard and fast until she could think of nothing but the aches in her legs and lungs.

Ranji sipped her cappuccino and said, 'You wanted to see me.'

The brain specialist from the university nodded. 'Indeed. Let me get straight to the point. I'm recruiting certain sorts of memory patient for a full-blown clinical trial. I thought there might be mutual benefit for you and me. And the patients. Can I tell you what I'm talking about?'

'I think you'd better.'

'Okay,' Professor Dench replied. 'My research group has come up with a way of modifying memories. We're the first in the world to do such a thing. Let me be clear. We're some way from implanting false memories into animal or human brains. What we've done is alter an existing memory. We let lab rats explore a new layout until they fall asleep. In their sleep, their brains replay their explorations of the new place to firm up their memory. I don't need to tell you this. You know that's how we all learn new things. Rats or humans. We rehearse in our sleep.

'Anyway, we put these rats in a brain scanner and watched while they slept. Whenever the place-cells lit up, we used electrodes to stimulate the rats' brains in an area associated with pleasure and reward. As soon as ones who'd had this treatment woke up, they made a dash for the new layout – because they remembered, wrongly of course, that they were rewarded for being there. The rats whose brains weren't tweaked didn't know what all the fuss was about and didn't bother with the layout at all.' He gazed at the head of the Institute for Memory Disorders. 'Memory successfully changed.'

'Interesting,' said Ranji. She waved a hand towards the mug in front of him. 'Don't let your coffee go cold.'

'With this sort of intervention, I might be able to make myself adore cold coffee.'

'Even I can think of more important uses than that. Are you saying you've tried it with humans?'

'A few, yes. There's a woman with a severe phobia of spiders. We forced her to interact with them and then tweaked her pleasure centres when her sleeping brain replayed the horrific experience. Afterwards, for her, it was horrific no more. Now, she keeps spiders as pets. Fifty-eight at the last count, she tells me. Then there's the most common fear: heights. The man I treated goes climbing now. And a boy with an extreme fear of buttons. He hadn't been to school for ages – and hardly ever left his house. Crippling. Anyway, he had the same treatment and now he's back in uniform, doing up his own shirts, going to school normally. No longer terrified. It's a joy to see the improvement.

'But these are just anecdotes. What I really need is a proper human trial, with volunteers.'

Ranji nodded. 'If, say, a youngster has suffered abuse or some sort of trauma … '

'Yes. We can soften the memory. A brain scan will soon tell us when they're replaying the painful memories in their sleep. We'd stimulate their reward centres and that would take away the negative emotions.'

'Do *you* suffer any phobias or stress-related problems?'

The neuroscientist smiled. 'I know where you're going with this. No, I don't. But, if I did, I'd get in line. Yes, I'd volunteer. It's all been cleared by the Ethics Committee. In fact … '

'What?'

'The button boy.'

'Yes?'

'He's my son, Owen.'

'Ah. Okay. You must be confident in your method.'

'Yes, I am.'

'I can see the logic and value of what you do,' said

Ranji. 'But most of the people coming to my institute have lost their memories. I only have a few with the opposite problem of too many – and traumatic ones. Most of them respond to cognitive behavioural therapy. No brain surgery is needed, just talking to an expert.'

'You said *most*. What about the ones that don't respond to CBT?'

'Would I volunteer any of my patients? Well, I have a reservation but … Maybe.'

'If you're interested, we can talk through your reservation now – or some other time.'

Ranji finished her coffee and glanced at her watch. 'I have to get back to an appointment. Presumably you've got some details to leave with me – bedtime reading – and contact details.'

Professor Dench handed over an article with a business card attached. 'You'd do me a favour if you'd go through it. More important, you might well do a difficult patient a favour.'

'Okay. Thanks.'

Professor Dench took a sip of coffee and then stood up. Leaving half of it in the mug, he strode back to the university.

Shifting her tactics for a final time, Dr Nawaz said, 'Hey. Here's an idea, Sophie. One of the nurses likes jogging.

You're good at running. I've seen you. Do you want to go out for a run with her?'

Sophie nodded.

After a month of daily runs, Ranji's assistant did not report any progress, any baring of Sophie's soul. The only thing Ranji learned was that Sophie was a much better runner than the nurse.

Ranji checked her watch and the nameplate on the door, knocked, and walked into Professor Dench's office. She nodded. 'Hello again.'

Professor Dench glanced at the clock on the wall and noted that the head of the Institute for Memory Disorders was exactly on time. Looking eager, he waved her towards a chair. 'Good to see you.'

'Months ago,' she said, 'you told me to contact you if I had a patient who might benefit from your memory softening.'

'Yes?'

'It's a girl. Her name used to be Sophie Clinkard. Now she's Sophie Lightwing – and twelve years old. Nearly thirteen. At eight, she saw a domestic incident. Well, she saw lots of abuse – father on mother – but she was eight when she saw the worst.'

'Specifically?'

Ranji said, 'Her father let fly with an iron when her mother burnt a hole in his best shirt.'

After years of working with brains, Professor Dench was no longer surprised by any human behaviour. He hardly raised an eyebrow. 'He didn't do the ironing himself, then.'

'Apparently not. His one and only use of an iron was to batter his wife to death.'

'And that's what Sophie saw at eight?'

'She heard some shouting and went to take a look. It's still as fresh to her today as it was four years ago. She's in a constant state of suppressed fear.'

'Poor kid.'

'She's been brutalised by it – mentally – and she's reacted by detaching herself from the world and normal behaviour.'

'I'm not surprised.'

'She couldn't explain at first – not in words – but the pictures she drew were clear enough. Since then, she's had an extensive course of CBT for trauma, but … ' Ranji shrugged.

'No significant improvement?'

'Water off a duck's back.'

'You've got full medical notes?'

'They remain confidential for the moment.'

'Of course, but if she became part of my trial … '

'Then, yes.'

Professor Dench said, 'I gather she's been adopted.'

'A family environment to provide nurture and stability.'

'Her biological father's locked up?'

'For a long, long time. Perhaps forever. As I said, it wasn't his first offence.'

A grim smile formed on the professor's face. 'Barred from the laundry room – and the ironing – I hope.'

Ranji returned the expression. 'Well? Is she the sort of case you might be able to help?'

'I'd need to see those notes, but I think so. With the approval of her adoptive parents.'

'What about my approval?'

'Technically, I don't need it. It's down to the patient and, because she's young, her guardians. The Ethics Committee's already approved it. But … '

'Yes?'

'I hope you'd give it your blessing.'

'Well, here's the thing,' Ranji replied. 'I'm not sure I can.'

'Ah. That reservation you mentioned? But you're here. You must be contemplating going for it.'

'I'm here because I'd be failing my patient if I didn't find out all possible ways forward and put them to the family. It doesn't mean I'd recommend every one. If someone said acupuncture would help, I'd tell the parents – along with my assessment of its worth.'

'So, what's bothering you?'

Ranji took a breath. 'It's this. Everyone's identity is built on a collection of memories. I'm the person who got chickenpox at the age of four and fell off my bike and smashed a tooth at eight. I saw my favourite grandad die of a heart attack when I was twelve and stumbled over my marriage vows. Happy or sad, they're my memories. No one else has the same ones. They make me who I am. As painful as it might be, I have to learn to live with the bad ones. Interfere with that – take away the trauma – and I become someone else, someone who wasn't affected by the bad things. In other words, change someone's memory – for whatever reason – and you change their identity.'

'Perhaps your patient – Sophie – *needs* change. Time hasn't healed her. Talking therapies haven't. She might welcome the sort of change you're talking about. You wouldn't welcome it because you're not damaged like her. I think it'd be a good thing to damp down her memories. The painful ones. Give her a chance at a life not crippled by trauma.'

Ranji had first met Grace and Tony Lightwing as part of the vetting procedure before Sophie was adopted. Now, she was seeing them again out of a duty to her patient. Even if she didn't fully approve of Professor Dench's procedure, she felt compelled to bring it to the attention of Sophie's parents. Their experience with a damaged, adopted child had already had its effect. Slumped in office chairs, Grace Lightwing looked worn and Tony Lightwing was undoubtedly frazzled. They needed to see a faint flicker of light ahead. They needed a way of improving Sophie's prognosis.

'There's a neuroscientist at the university who offers the most radical and experimental option,' she told them. 'That doesn't mean I'm recommending it. I just need to inform you about it so you can make your own decision. A man called Professor Dench … '

She outlined his research, what it entailed, the benefits for the few human subjects so far, and his need for more patients to make a proper clinical trial of the procedure. 'If you're interested, Professor Dench would tell you a lot more.' Ranji looked at the relief on the Lightwings' faces and knew already that they would enrol Sophie in the trial.

'But,' Ranji added, 'I see a downside to what he does. You need to think about this. Memories – good and not so good – make us what we are. Our understanding of ourselves depends on remembering our pasts. Take me. My memories belong to me and no one else has the same ones, so they make me unique. They make me *me*. Change our memories and *we're* changed. So this is the question. Is Sophie ready to be changed? Are you prepared for her to be changed?'

'Absolutely,' Mr Lightwing replied without hesitation.

'She deserves a better future than the one she's got,' Mrs Lightwing agreed. 'We'd try anything to make sure that happens.'

'How do we contact this professor?' Tony asked.

Methodically, Professor Dench's assistants prepared the operating theatre, the equipment and themselves for the next troubled volunteer. In the adjacent room, the professor smiled at his young patient. She seemed totally unruffled but she cowered away from him. 'You know what's going to happen, don't you, Sophie? We talked about it. There's nothing at all to worry about. We're just going to pin nice thoughts onto a nasty memory. Change the emotional association. And, to do that, we're going to implant a couple of tiny electrodes into your brain for a while. One in a part of your memory centre, the other in the rewards centre. Sorry, Sophie,' he said, reaching out towards her long hair, 'but this has got to come off first.'

Sophie recoiled and then shrugged.

'It's going to work like this. When I've got the electrodes in place, you'll go into an MRI scanner – a brain scanner. When you think back to what happened in your old living room, we'll see what parts light up. Afterwards, when you're asleep, your brain will be thinking about what happened. The same bits will light up and I'll attach nice feelings to it – a reward – instead. And that's it. Done. I take the electrodes out and you carry on as if nothing's happened. Except that I think you'll be a lot happier.'

The professor nodded at Mr and Mrs Lightwing and then at the nurse with a razor in her hand. 'I'm going to go next door and check everything's ready. Okay? It's all going to be very straightforward.'

11

The sports club was full of weekend warriors – adults who used Saturdays and Sundays to binge on exercising. They were easy to spot. Sweat oozed from every pore. Their cotton tops were blotched with large dark stains. Watch a weekend warrior for long enough and the dewy patches expanded and coalesced, making one soggy, smelly mess. Really, Sophie and Jonah decided, there should be a club rule forbidding weekend warriors from loitering anywhere but beside air-conditioning vents. Sophie even spotted a middle-aged overweight warrior with an ever-spreading damp patch around the crotch of his shorts. Nodding towards him, she whispered to Jonah, 'I hope that's only sweat.'

Jonah grinned. 'Too much cotton. Next time, he'll buy Lycra.'

'Yeah. Then we'll see it leaking down his legs instead.'

Jonah's phone chirped with an incoming message. 'That'll be Mum and Dad's spreadsheet.'

'What?'

'It always arrives about this time on a Sunday.'

'But what is it?'

'Their schedule for the week.'

'They send you a spreadsheet of what they're up to?'

Jonah fiddled with his phone. 'I'll show you. Look. Mum's red and Dad's blue. Sunday – today – they're both about to leave for the hospital. Tomorrow after school, Dad'll be home but Mum's working a late shift. On Tuesday, both of them will be home in the evening.'

'What's the yellow, starting Wednesday?'

'I'm yellow. I'm on a school trip from Wednesday to Friday. We're going to some place in the south called London.'

'Never heard of it.'

'Nor me. I'll tell you what it's like when I get back.'

Sophie examined the spreadsheet again. 'So, you have to tell your mum and dad what you're doing each week? In advance.'

'No. They just put in any specials – like school trips. See? On Wednesday I'm away, Mum's off work at seven, but Dad's on duty till ten.'

'Amazing.'

Jonah shrugged. 'They're doctors,' he said, as if that explained everything.

'But it means after we're done here, you've got an empty house.'

'Yes.'

'What are we waiting for?'

Jonah gave her a sidelong glance. 'We get along pretty well, you and me, but … you make it sound like you're from some crazy we-can-convert-them-to-the-straight-side organisation.'

'It was the empty house I fancied, not you.'

'Thanks.'

'Come on.' She slapped his arm. 'You heard my trainer. Finish with five minutes at eighty per cent, one minute's walk, five minutes at ninety per cent, one minute's walk, and five minutes at a hundred per cent – or more. After that, I get at least a minute's rest, waiting for you to catch up.'

On the far side of the perimeter track, the furthest point from the pavilion, Sophie was running at ninety per cent of her capacity, rapidly closing the gap on a weekend warrior. Plainly, the woman ahead heard Sophie's footfalls and unwisely looked round. She twisted awkwardly and seemed to trip over her own feet. She fell and her head crashed against a railing. At once, the blood flowed.

Sophie wound down, stopped and, eager to see the damage, knelt beside the jogger. 'Are you okay?'

Dazed, the woman said, 'I'm fine.' She put her hand up to her head and it came away deep red. 'Oh. Perhaps … '

She didn't look fine to Sophie. Her eyes weren't focusing properly. Sophie said, 'You need help.'

Gasping, Jonah ran up to them and slowed to a halt.

Sophie looked up at him and said, 'Well? Your parents are doctors. You should know what to do.'

'I don't think it works like that.'

'We need a bandage. One of us has got to whip their top off – and it sure isn't going to be me.'

'All right,' Jonah replied, yanking off his shirt.

Licking her lips, Sophie mopped up as much blood as she could with Jonah's polyester top, but it wasn't very absorbent. Then she folded it over and over until it was a long thin strip. Enjoying the contact with the wounded warrior, she positioned the makeshift bandage over the gash and tied the two ends tightly behind the woman's head.

'We'll walk you back to the centre. Make sure you're okay.'

'Thanks.'

Sophie's heart was beating fast, as if she were still running at ninety per cent. Now, though, the cause wasn't exertion. It was excitement. She found great pleasure in dealing with the head wound.

Taking a hand each, Sophie and Jonah pulled the woman upright.

'You look cool,' Sophie said to her. 'Like wearing … what's that thing called?'

'A bandana?' Jonah suggested.

'Yes. A bandana. Pity about the bloodstains. Not a good fashion statement.' But strangely appealing to Sophie.

The woman smiled drunkenly. 'I couldn't believe how fast you came up behind me. You're a phenomenal runner.'

'Never mind about me,' Sophie replied. 'Just concentrate on walking.'

After they had escorted the wounded weekend warrior to the medical room, Sophie turned to Jonah. 'I never did get up to a hundred per cent. That's the best bit. Let's fire the afterburners and run full pelt to your place.'

Jonah gulped. 'Do you ever stop?'

'For meals and sleep, yes.'

Sophie waited on the porch of Jonah's empty house. Jonah arrived after a while and said, 'I should've given you the key – except you would've set the alarm off.' He unlocked and opened the front door. Immediately, the alarm let out urgent beeps. Sophie followed him inside and shut the door, noticing that it was the type that locked automatically. With Sophie standing behind him,

Jonah cancelled the burglar alarm by entering the code on a keypad.

They didn't do much with a house devoid of authority. They played some games, watched a downloaded programme on 10km runners, streamed some music, and talked about parents, boys and school. But it didn't matter to Sophie. Her day was working out perfectly. Soon, she ran home.

12

It was Monday morning. Summoned to Sophie's school, Grace Lightwing had absented herself from work for an hour. With a puzzled and concerned expression, she sat down opposite the headteacher.

'Thanks for coming in, Mrs Lightwing. I thought we needed to speak face-to-face, but it's not a huge issue, so don't worry about it.' The headteacher shuffled in her seat before plunging in. 'Last week, Thursday, I had occasion to discipline one of the girls in Sophie's class. Nothing important, nothing too serious. A few stern words, a token punishment and it was done. Or so I thought. On Friday, though, the girl's mother turned up to complain. She wasn't complaining about how I'd dealt with her daughter, but rather about consistency and fairness. And I think she has a point.'

'Oh?'

'Her argument went like this. There are a lot of school rules, and once a student has broken one of them a couple of times, I get involved and something happens about it. Except in the case of your daughter. This mother told me that it was common knowledge that Sophie is treated with kid gloves – as if it's one rule for everybody else and a different rule for Sophie.'

'What rule are we talking about?'

'It could be any, but the most obvious one is no running along the corridors. Sophie probably breaks that rule five times a day. And I've checked. The school – I – have never done anything about it. This girl's mother came here to say that, if Sophie had been any other student, she would've been in trouble many times over.' The headteacher shrugged. 'She's right. I know why we're wary of tackling Sophie. We have no wish to add to her considerable burden, but it's my job to see the bigger picture – to think of all the other students and the effect on them of seeing Sophie let off over and over again.'

Grace nodded. 'I understand.'

'She's doing much better now, isn't she? None of the meltdowns we used to have.'

'That's right.'

'As far as I see it, she's developed into a stable, strong character. An asset to the school. She has a few good friends and she'd have more if it weren't for this perceived favouritism.'

'I sense the punchline's coming.'

The headteacher smiled. 'I think she's got to be treated like everyone else. No more kid gloves. Ultimately it'll be good for her – once she gets used to it. If she does something wrong, she's subject to the same discipline as everyone else.' The headteacher paused. 'Are you happy to support this decision?'

'It sounds fair.'

'Good.' The headteacher stood up. 'You could help by talking it through with her tonight. Tomorrow morning, I'll tell the staff we've got a new approach.'

Grace also got to her feet. 'Okay.'

13

It was easy enough for Sophie to figure out who'd complained. Verity Wilson had copped it from the staff at the end of last week. It wasn't Verity's fault that the school was suddenly gunning for her, though. Verity was okay, but her mother – a school bus driver – was a different matter altogether.

'Oh, I know,' Sophie said, agreeing with Jonah as he flung clothes into a holdall on Tuesday evening. 'No one should get special treatment, but … '

'But what?'

'The school makes a big thing about how good I am at running. It's a bit weird when they tell me off for running. You'd think they could look the other way.'

'Sounds like they did – till today.'

Not in the best of moods, Sophie sighed.

Jonah's father called up the stairs, 'Have you got your bedroom door open, like we said?'

'Yes,' Jonah shouted back. He turned to Sophie, raised his eyebrows and shook his head.

'Well, don't take your front door key with you to London. I hate to think where it'd end up. Leave it here – out of sight.'

'All right.' Jonah dropped the key into the top drawer of his bedside cabinet and continued to pack.

Later, when he went to the toilet, Sophie wrapped a hankie around her right hand, plucked the key back out of the drawer, and slipped it into her pocket.

When Mr and Mrs Quinn invited them into the living room, Sophie got the impression that the drinks and cakes on the table were a bribe to stop them being on their own and out of sight in Jonah's bedroom.

Taking one of the buns, Sophie muttered, 'It's okay. I'm his girlfriend only in the sense that I'm a friend who happens to be a girl.'

'Oh. I see.'

'It's not going any further than that, if you're wondering.' She looked in turn at his parents. 'It can't.'

'Why do you say that?'

Knowing that Sophie was in a strange mood, Jonah stared at her, silently panicking that she was about to out him.

'Because I'm gay,' Sophie announced.

'Gay?' Mrs Quinn was clearly shocked. Appalled.

'Yes, it means I'm a normal girl who just happens to fall for other girls.'

Mr Quinn spluttered, 'But … '

'What?'

'It's not natural,' Mr Quinn said, disgust written all over his face.

'It's perfectly natural,' Sophie replied. 'There are lots of us. At least one in every hundred. And quite a few animals keep to same-sex relationships as well. You can't say wild animals aren't acting naturally.'

'I think you'd better leave,' Mrs Quinn said, as if Sophie had some grotesque, infectious disease.

'It's not catching, you know.'

'Right now.'

'What? Even before I've finished my chocolate mint cupcake?'

'Yes.'

Sophie shrugged. 'All right.'

At the front door, Jonah said in an urgent whisper, 'Why did you do that?'

She smiled. 'I just wanted to see if they're as bad as you thought they'd be. They are.' Half-way down the path, she called out happily, 'Have a good trip. See you after.'

14

After school on Wednesday, Sophie put in a couple of hours' training. Then she left her phone in her locker at the sports club. Still wearing her all-over running gear and gloves, she headed at speed for Jonah's house, her heart thumping agreeably in her chest. Apart from her head, her skin was completely covered in Lycra. Her hair was tucked inside the beanie hat she wore for running in cold weather.

Jonah's key was already in her gloved hand as she approached his front door. She didn't delay. Didn't think twice. Within seconds, she was inside and out of view. The burglar alarm was spitting out its warning. Sophie headed for the keypad and typed in the code that she'd seen Jonah enter. At once, the system relaxed to silence, convinced that there was no stranger danger.

Sophie glanced at the clock in the hallway and smiled. Six thirty-five.

She had worked it all out beforehand. Even so, she needed to think clearly, methodically. She went straight upstairs to Jonah's room, opened his top drawer and replaced the door key. She positioned it carefully – exactly where Jonah had left it. From start to finish, it had not come into contact with her skin.

Then she tiptoed along to the Quinns' bedroom. A large room with lots of mirrors, cupboards, luxuriously soft carpet, and a sumptuous double bed. The duvet was a startling red and gold. Fit for royalty. The first wardrobe contained only Mrs Quinn's clothes. Neat rows of proper posh outfits, mostly new, all fashionable. Sophie closed the door on the extravagant display. Using only the remains of the evening's natural light, she slid open the second wardrobe. She'd guessed correctly; it was full of Mr Quinn's clothing. His trousers, shirts and jackets were organised impeccably, like a Dulux colour chart. The shirts began at pure white and ran through every shade to dark blue. His trousers were graded in perfect sequence from light grey to jet black. Sophie smiled and shook her head. First, she scanned the line of immaculately pressed shirts. She selected one of the light colours, so it would show any stains. Light blue. Next, she selected some trousers – a boring beige – and a darker jacket. None of them would fit her snugly, but it didn't matter. It mattered only that she could wear them, however ridiculous they looked and felt over her running gear.

With a top layer of Mr Quinn's clothes, Sophie examined herself in one of the full-length mirrors and grinned at the sight. She looked like a company manager who had unaccountably shrunk since getting dressed. A little like a clown. But a clown with serious intent.

Satisfied, she went back downstairs. Her spine shivered with pleasure as she stepped into the living room and reached out for that glass lion. Weighing the heavy ornament in her gloved hand, it felt perfect. The shape, the mass, the density, everything. Perfect.

Sophie's brain had been reprogrammed. The torture of bad memories had been erased. Now, thoughts of a weapon, of violence, of the death of a mother brought an irresistible gush of nice feelings, an overwhelming reward. Like a drug, it had to be repeated. And here she was doing her friend a favour at the same time. Actually, it went beyond Jonah. Knowing that Mr and Mrs Quinn were such bigots, she was doing the whole world a favour.

She checked her watch. Seven o'clock. The time the first Dr Quinn was due to leave the hospital. She could arrive in just a few minutes. Sophie went to the walk-in utility cupboard off the hall. It was an ideal place to wait while staying out of sight. Keeping the glass lion in her right hand, she drew in the door with her left. She didn't close it completely, though. From inside the snug space, she peered through the crack and readied herself, as if on the start line. Just like a race, what was about to happen would test her to the limit, but it would also be hugely enjoyable.

She predicted a personal best.

The house was eerily quiet and suddenly dark. Dusk had obliterated the last sunlight and the only noises came from the central heating. The boiler made a slight hum – a vibration – and there were occasional creaks as the pipes and radiators warmed and expanded.

Sophie didn't mind the wait. Anticipation would make the action even sweeter when it came. Besides, there was no rush. She would have three hours before the second Dr Quinn set out for home. In fact, she wished she had less time.

A car engine. A glow swept across the hall like a lighthouse beam. Headlights. A rumble as the garage door opened, and again as it closed. A key in the lock, the front door opening, the hall light abruptly blazing.

Sophie shuffled silently, eagerly, from foot to foot. Through the narrow gap, she watched Mrs Quinn. Standing beside the alarm's control box, checking out the display, Jonah's mum looked surprised and annoyed that the last person to leave the house had not primed the burglar alarm. Making a tutting noise, Mrs Quinn stripped off her coat and hung it on a hook in the hall. Then she slipped out of her shoes and made for the kitchen. She was out of Sophie's line of sight, but Sophie could tell from the noises that she was making herself a hot drink.

Cup in hand, Mrs Quinn came past the crack in the door and went into the living room. That was Sophie's cue. She couldn't help herself any more. Adrenalin was surging through her body, she was tingling with excitement. Treading softly on the plush carpet, she made for the same room. Just as she stretched out her left arm towards the door, she hesitated as Mrs Quinn's mobile phone burst into life.

'Everything okay?' she asked.

Sophie couldn't hear the reply.

'Oh. That's a surprise. A nice surprise.'

'Trade in a couple of hours now for a couple in the morning? Why not? Sounds good to me. But it's up to you.'

'Okay. I'll see you soon, then. Bye.'

Sophie guessed that Mr Quinn was going to make his entrance much sooner than she expected. That suited her, as long as she still had time to deal with Mrs Quinn. She burst into the living room.

Jonah's mum jumped up in fright. Her sudden movement launched the teacup a short distance across the room, slopping deep brown liquid over the carpet. The saucer remained in her hand. 'You!' she exclaimed. Briefly, puzzled, she glanced down at her husband's ill-fitting clothes on the intruder.

Sophie had the element of surprise on her side. She raised her right arm high and brought it down with all her strength, glass first, on to Mrs Quinn's forehead.

There was a sound like a shoe cracking the ice of a frozen puddle. Just as the pressure from the foot would bring water to the surface, forcing it up through the smashed crust and over the shoe, Sophie's heavy blow brought a gush of warm blood to the cracked bone, over her hand and the glass lion. A joyful release. It sprayed liberally onto the clothes that Sophie was wearing. Mrs Quinn just stood there, swaying slightly, unfocused, open-mouthed. The saucer fell from her hand to the carpet. She collapsed only when Sophie delivered the second jubilant strike.

To make sure, Sophie smashed the ornament down four more times. Each gleeful impact – glass on skull – took away more of Mrs Quinn's warped humanity. A humanity that this particular mother didn't deserve. Each lunge fixed a bad attitude. Each one was a lesson that would be learned. Each one repaid a mistake that would never ever be repeated. Each one was a triumph for Jonah.

In her mind, Sophie heard Jonah talking about that ridiculous parental spreadsheet. 'Mum's red,' his voice said in her mind. Sophie looked down at her handiwork and grinned. 'Sure is.'

Posh blood looked exactly the same as ordinary blood. It ran just as freely, just as jauntily. The sight gave Sophie such a high. The tingle blossomed in her brain until she experienced ecstasy. Her body was a riot of feel-good hormones. Endorphins and oxytocin. Absolute bliss.

She no longer had three hours to relish the sensation, to celebrate the occasion. Mr Quinn could be on his way at any moment. Calmly, she removed Mr Quinn's soiled clothes and stuffed them into the log burner. Using a firelighter and a match from the box on the mantelpiece, Sophie made a half-hearted attempt to burn the clothes, making sure enough was left for the forensic team to find, identify and analyse the blood spatter pattern.

In the downstairs toilet, she washed away a small trickle of blood on her face and the stains on her right glove and left shoe. Then she was done. Elated, she put her head out of the front door and looked around. It was dark and, in such a leafy suburb, it was very unlikely that anyone would see her leave. Anyway, no one took notice of road runners any more. She was about to make her move when headlights appeared from the right, probing the road a few metres ahead of a slow-moving car. Wondering if Mr Quinn was about to arrive, Sophie ducked back inside and waited. Her heartrate increased as if she were inside the final kilometre. But, no, the engine noise did not change. It merely dwindled as the car rolled past.

Sophie opened the door a crack. This time, headlights came from the left and the car was decelerating. Sophie heard the change of tone as the car turned into the Quinns' drive. The headlight beam swung across the lawn, the tyres clattered over the stones and the engine revved as Mr Quinn headed for the double garage at the other end of the house. The door lifted up automatically as the car approached. As soon as it disappeared inside and the headlights dimmed, Sophie stepped outside, pulled the front door shut quietly and sprinted away down the path with a broad smile on her face.

Done. Two bigots with one statue.

She went home via the sports club so she could pick up her mobile.

15

Sgt AJ Yorke
Ref 2019/09/0148/QUI

NOTES

Mr Peter Quinn left work (general hospital) and went home early.
Phoned his wife (Florence Quinn) first. 19.14.
Found the house locked. About 19.45.
Found his wife in living room, already dead.
Being a doctor, he confirmed death, then called police. 19.51.
Confirmed remains of bloodstained clothes in log burner were his.
20.35.
Denied all knowledge of how they got there.
Denied trying to destroy clothes.
Denied murdering his wife.
No sign of forced entry.

Burglar alarm in working condition, not tampered with.
Son (Jonah Quinn) away on school trip.

16

Forensic examination and pathology
Ref 2019/09/0148/QUI

SUMMARY

Death of Florence Quinn caused by severe head trauma; six blows by glass ornament in shape of a lion; two blows delivered with victim upright; four delivered while prone.

Time of death consistent with arrival of Peter Quinn (husband of victim) at crime scene.

Attempt to burn bloodstained clothing belonging to Peter Quinn unsuccessful. Sufficient material remained for testing: (a) blood on clothing belonged to victim; (b) blood spatter pattern entirely consistent with the six strikes; (c) skin fragments on clothing belonged to Peter Quinn.

Several non-incriminating fingerprints in victim's house, including prints matching those in Case Ref

2019/08/0124/HOP (accidental death of Carmen Hope), identified as Sophie Lightwing.

Smudged fingerprints on weapon belong to Peter Quinn and victim only.

DNA on weapon belongs to Peter Quinn and victim only.

Victim holding saucer and cup of tea at the time of attack. No other fingerprints on crockery.

No evidence of intruders.

17

'It's quite a coincidence, isn't it?' Zena Kirkland, the Senior Investigating Officer on the Quinn case, put her head on one side and raised her prominently painted eyebrows.

Sergeant Lightwing shrugged. 'Just one of those things.'

'It's perturbing, though, your Sophie being linked to both cases. Carmen Hope and now Florence Quinn. Her friends' parents seem to suffer a lot of bad luck. Very odd.'

'One was an accident. The other's a clear-cut domestic. Husband on wife. Anyway,' Tony said, 'Sophie was at her sports club – in it or running nearby when it happened.'

'I know. I had her phone record checked.' The SIO sighed. 'I've got no reason to doubt her, no reason to talk to her. No reason to regard her as a suspect. But … something's niggling me, Tony.'

'What?'

'I looked up what happened to Sophie's biological mother. Ben Clinkard hit her six times with an iron. Six times. Florence Quinn took the same – six hits.'

'With an ornament, not an iron.'

'Even so … '

Tony Lightwing shrugged again. 'Another coincidence, that's all. It can't be anything else. Sophie wouldn't – *couldn't* – have done anything like that. For one thing, she couldn't have got past the locked front door and the burglar alarm. No traces of her on the weapon. And she was nowhere near the crime scene. On top of that, she was getting on really well with Jonah Quinn. I saw it with my own eyes. So, no motive.'

'Was she getting on really well with his parents?'

'As far as I know. She visited at least a couple of times. Ask Jonah.'

'I did. Nothing. I got the impression he preferred Sophie to his mum and dad. He certainly wasn't going to say anything that put her in a bad light.' Detective Inspector Kirkland changed the subject. 'Did I hear you'd made enquiries about getting Sophie some work experience in forensics?'

Tony nodded.

'She's interested in forensic science, then.'

'So are a lot of kids her age.'

Zena smiled. 'That's true. It's the blood and gore that does it. They wouldn't be so keen if they knew it was analysing for alcohol and examining paint flakes all the time.'

18

Jonah ran and ran until he couldn't run any more. Eyes and nose streaming, he collapsed in an untidy heap. He heaved, cried and groaned all at once.

Sophie sat beside him on the grass and said, 'That's the fastest I've seen you go.'

'I wasn't doing it for speed,' he spluttered. 'I did it to give me something else to think about.'

'Did it work?'

'Not now I've stopped.' He wiped his face on his sleeve. 'My dad's been arrested.'

'And charged,' Sophie added. 'My dad told me.' She paused before asking, 'Do you think he did it?'

'There's no other explanation. Nothing else makes any sense. He says he didn't, though.'

'Well, he would, wouldn't he?' Sophie looked at her running mate and said, 'Sorry.'

Jonah took a few deep breaths. 'It's like your friend, Elizabeth, and what happened to her mum.'

'No, it isn't. That was an accident.'

Jonah looked away.

'Where are you living?' Sophie said.

'With my uncle. My dad's brother.'

'That could be awkward.'

Jonah shook his head. 'They never got on. Dad and Uncle Ian. Once – ages ago – I remember something Uncle Ian said. It's stuck with me but I didn't know what he meant back then. He said, "When the time comes for you to talk about who you are, best not do it with your dad. Or your mum. Come to me. All right?"'

Sophie exclaimed, 'He knows!'

'Guess so. Don't know how, though.'

'And he's okay with it.'

Jonah nodded. 'That's the feeling I get.'

Sophie fisted the air. 'That means it's all worked out fine.'

Jonah dragged himself upright and said, 'I need to run some more.'

A few of the girls at school were clustered in front of the computer screen. Verity Wilson said, 'Watch this. Boys! They nicked an old lady's car at Morrisons. Drove off in it while she was taking her trolley back. No seatbelts, of course. And, to make it worse, they filmed themselves doing it.'

As the car slithered onto the main road, one of the boys was going through the shopping bag on back seat. Whoever was next to him was recording it all on his phone. 'Look, she's bought a fish.' He held it up. 'Slimy.' The wobbly camera zoomed in on it and back out again. It was clear that the driver had little control. The car bounced over a pavement at speed and careered back into the road. The boy by the shopping bag held the fish by its tail fin and slapped the driver on the back of his head with it. The car lurched, crashed into a concrete bollard and came to an immediate halt. The driver's airbag blew up and pinned him into his seat. The passenger's airbag must have been deactivated. The other boy in the front didn't come to an immediate halt. Momentum carried him forward. His head smacked into the windscreen, creating a splash of blood. It was followed by a fresh mackerel.

The picture went spinning out of focus as the two boys in the back also flew forwards. On the soundtrack, there were three loud thuds and two yelps of pain.

'Gross!' a girl called Ursula Graham cried.

'Stupid!'

'Love the fish.'

'Ouch!'

Transfixed, Sophie watched the slow-motion clip of the boy's head hitting the glass and the spreading crimson pattern. She pretended to be appalled as well, but her brain operated on a different wavelength. Inside, she quivered with satisfaction.

Verity said, 'Sophie?' and moved away from Ursula and the rest of the group.

Sophie followed.

'I'm sorry about … you know … you getting nicked for running down the corridors.'

Sophie smiled. 'No problem.'

'It wasn't me who complained.'

'I'm guessing it was your mum.'

'Yeah. She's like that.'

'A bit of a cow sometimes?'

'Especially when she's been stuck in a traffic jam,' Verity replied.

Sophie smiled again. 'Isn't that every day?'

'Nearly.'

'I know she's at it between eight and nine and three and four, but what does she do for the rest of the day?'

'It's not just the school bus she drives,' said Verity. 'In between, she runs a community service.'

'What's that?'

'Driving old dears to the shops, the doctors or church. Or the community centre. She does other stuff as well. She's into old folk. Not so keen on us.'

Sophie nodded. Still feeling satisfied about how she'd helped Jonah, she began to work out how she could do something similar for Verity. Improving her friends' lives was a convenient justification for chasing the rapture.

That evening, Sophie sat down for dinner with her parents. Fish pie. Selecting a forkful of white flesh from amongst the mash, she said, 'If you can't get me a place in forensics, Dad, the school's looking for something in cars. Brakes, airbags, seatbelts and that sort of thing are cool.'

Her father's next mouthful was drenched in tomato ketchup. He hesitated before eating it. 'Oh. What brought that on?'

Unable to ignore fish pie, Pudding jumped up onto Sophie's lap and looked imploring at her plate.

'A talk on careers in engineering. I was interested in all the safety gadgets.'

'Why?'

She shrugged and shooed Pudding away. 'Why do you watch cricket?'

He smiled. 'Okay. I don't suppose any of us are much good at explaining why we like the things we do. You just took me by surprise, that's all.'

'Good idea,' her mum said. 'Show all those boys how it's done.'

'I just thought it'd be useful to find out how anti-crash stuff works,' said Sophie.

Her dad nodded. 'Cars might change a lot in the next few years. New technology and all that. They might even go driverless but safety features are here to stay.' He paused before adding, 'I'll keep trying in Forensics, but it's good to have a backup plan.'

Changing the subject, Grace said, 'Are you keeping in touch with Jonah? Poor lad. How's he getting on after … ?'

'He's okay. He's with an uncle. Working it out of his system by running – faster than ever.'

Deep in thought, Tony swallowed some salmon. He hesitated and then said, 'Rewind a bit.'

'What?'

'There's a branch of Forensics that deals with cars. Vehicles, I should say. You know, taking them apart if they've been involved in crime, looking for evidence or money, or what have you. Investigating traffic accidents. Checking in case they've been tampered with.'

'Perfect,' Grace said. 'The best of both worlds. Forensics *and* car safety.'

'Yeah,' Sophie replied, finally giving in and giving a piece of haddock to Pudding. 'Get me in there and I'm a happy bunny.'

19

Sophie's world had turned upside down. In the garage, she was lying on her back and powerful lamps built into the floor shone upwards so she could examine every part of the van's underside. Actually, she was there to observe rather than to do.

'Yep,' Mike said. 'There's something. See it? Next to the brake pipe.'

'The box?'

'Yep,' the forensic engineer repeated. 'Manufacturers don't bolt long metal boxes to the underneath of their vehicles. Someone else put it there.'

'What for? I mean, to carry something, obviously. But what's in it?'

'Something the owner didn't want us to know about. That's why he didn't stop when Customs told him to. Hence the chase and the crash. Let's take a look.'

They were wearing overalls, masks and gloves. Almost no part of them could come into contact with the suspect van. A camera recorded every move as Mike applied a spanner to the first of four nuts.

'Do you ever have cars or buses that have been sabotaged?' Sophie asked. 'You know. Tampered with.'

'Not these days,' Mike replied as he adjusted his position to work on the bolt. 'Are you thinking of those old films?'

'Which old films?'

'You know. The bad guy cuts through the brake pipe and the victim drives off. Down a hill, the brakes don't work. The car slams into a brick wall or a lake, or flies off a cliff or something, and that's that. Simple. Job done.' Putting down the first nut and moving on to the second, Mike shook his head and smiled. 'Doesn't ring a bell? You're too young. Anyway, it doesn't really happen any more. A smart car will warn you there's a problem with the brakes before you even get going. Even if it doesn't, there's a seat belt and an air bag to think about.'

He took a moment to concentrate on removing the second nut and starting to tackle the third. 'How does the bad guy cut through the brake pipe, deactivate the air bag *and* disable the seat belt without the driver noticing? No chance. Modern technology ruins another plot. Nowadays, this job's mainly about identifying cars and drivers, sorting out traffic accidents, examining paint flakes, looking for evidence like we're doing now.

Discovering contraband probably.' He paused and said, 'Nearly there. You hold the whole thing up while I undo the last nut. I don't want it to fall down. In this game, we're as careful as we can be.'

Sophie wriggled into position alongside the engineer and used both hands to prop up the long and narrow box. 'Ready,' she said.

'This is where we start taking bets. Drugs, money, weapons, cigarettes, body parts … '

'Body parts?'

'Usually animals. Ivory, rhino horn, tiger parts for traditional medicine. But it's usually drugs. Have you ever seen heroin or cocaine close up?'

'No.'

Mike unscrewed the last nut. The hidden case came away and Sophie felt its full weight for the first time. She had braced herself for something heavy but it wasn't. 'Oh. It's quite light,' she said.

'Put it down on the plastic sheet and we'll take a look. If it's empty, we'll still find out what it was used for. There's always a trace to analyse.'

They emerged from opposite sides of the van. Mike carried the box to a well-lit bench and set up the camera.

'You're right,' he said. 'Not much weight. And it's locked. Not a time for subtlety.' He took a hacksaw and began to cut through the metal around the lock. 'I hope your first one's not a dud. It'd be nice for you to come across something juicy.'

He was clearly used to forcing his way into containers that crooks didn't want him to access. He sawed expertly and precisely, cutting away the minimum area of metal that would bypass the lock. When he'd finished, he held between his gloved forefinger and thumb a metal plate containing the lock. He put it down and said, 'Here we go.' He lifted the lid.

It wasn't empty. At first, neither Sophie nor Mike realised what they were looking at. There were three rolls wrapped in waterproof polythene.

'What have we here?' Mike murmured. He picked out the first roll and made sure it was within camera range. 'Very light.' Carefully, he sliced through the polythene with a small sharp scalpel. Inside, there was a cardboard tube. Before Mike turned his attention to it, he laid out the wrapping for later examination. It wasn't like opening a birthday present. Everything was precious to the investigation and nothing went in the bin.

At each end of the tube, there were plastic caps. Mike prized one away with his thumbs and again placed it on the clean surface of the bench. Then he peered inside. 'A roll of paper or something like. Quite thick.'

'A poster?' Sophie suggested. 'They come in tubes sometimes.'

'Maybe.' He inserted two gloved fingers into the tube and pulled out the rolled-up object. Even more cautiously, he unfurled it to reveal a very old oil painting on canvas. A fragile sailing ship tossed by an angry sea under a dark and threatening cloud.

'That's a surprise,' he muttered. 'A nice surprise. Smuggled artwork. Probably stolen and destined for a dodgy dealer or collector. It might be worth millions for all I know. I need a specialist. Grab me that evidence bag, will you? Make it safe till an expert can identify it.' He beamed at his trainee. 'You're lucky to see something special – not boring old drugs – on your first case.'

'Yeah.'

Sealing the painting in the evidence bag, Mike peered into the metal box again. 'Fancy seeing a couple more? Maybe it'll be a Mona Lisa with an enigmatic smile or an abstract masterpiece. Who knows?'

Sophie thought Mike was more enthralled than she was, but she played along. 'Okay. Let's see.'

The second oil painting showed a bunch of red and yellow flowers in a vase. Even if it was amazingly expensive, it didn't impress Sophie. She responded to the final piece, though. When Mike unrolled it, Sophie gasped at the vivid, jarring pastels painted on thin card. Under a blood-red sky, beside a messy swirl of dark sea, a sexless figure clasped both hands to the sides of an abstract face. There was real shock and pain here. A panic attack. Immediately, Sophie recognised someone experiencing a moment of utter dread, letting out a silent scream. Or maybe the figure was reacting against the infinite scream of nature, trying to stop it penetrating the ears.

Recovering her composure, Sophie muttered, 'I know that.'

Thinking she meant the image rather than the feeling, Mike said, 'It's one everyone knows. Edvard Munch – if it's genuine. I can't believe I'm holding *The Scream*. One of, anyway. I think he painted a few different versions of it. Astonishing.' Mike was in awe of the find. 'I'm as close to it as Munch when he painted it. Just imagine.'

Sophie was imagining a character caught in the instant between a brutal blow to the head and the gush of blood. A pleasant shiver ran from her brain down her spine.

'It's been stolen at least a couple of times – and recovered,' Mike told her, his gaze still fixed on the startling image. 'Looks like it's happened again.' He shook his head. 'I've got a great job. And that's a great result.'

20

Detective Inspector Zena Kirkland sat in front of her computer and scanned for unexpected deaths in the previous two years. She was looking for any fatal incident involving a parent, particularly a mother, with a child who might have known Sophie Lightwing.

As SIO of the Quinn case, Zena would normally have given the task to a member of her team, but she didn't want to create a crisis of loyalty within the ranks. If she'd announced this line of enquiry, she would have forced her staff to decide between their commitment to a confidential case and their allegiance to a fellow officer. Not wanting any leaks to reach Tony Lightwing, she did the work herself. She continued to scrutinise every database for deaths in unusual circumstances and then to check for links with the sergeant's daughter.

Apart from the Carmen Hope case, she found nothing.

21

A drink carton skidded crazily along the surface of the playground and the wrapper from a chocolate bar flew erratically with the wind. After her brief work experience, Sophie had returned to school. Sheltering from the squall in the Science Block, she said to Verity, 'I've been told off by the Head again, thanks to your mum.'

'Running down the corridors?'

Sophie nodded. 'First day back.'

Verity shrugged helplessly.

'Do you actually like her?'

'My mum?'

'Yeah.'

Verity laughed. 'Most of the time she's a pain. Aren't they all? Sometimes she's okay.'

The door shook and rattled, obstinately resisting the wind's attempts to prise it open.

'You said she does other stuff – apart from drive buses.'

'Why the interest?'

It was Sophie's turn to shrug. 'Just curious.'

'She looks after old people's gardens.'

'How do you mean?'

'You know. The ones who can't take care of their own any more. She mows their lawns, trims hedges, digs up weeds. All sorts of stuff. She calls herself the Lady Gardener.' Verity fished around in her bag. 'Look. I designed her business card.'

Sophie took the card and examined it. The profile of the woman looked like the image on the door of a public toilet but she was holding a chainsaw and standing next to a tree. Her business name was at the top and contact details were printed along the bottom. 'It's not a charity thing, then. Not something she volunteers for.'

'No. She does it for extra cash.'

Satisfied, Sophie nodded. 'You said she likes the old 'uns.'

'Yeah.'

Sophie pocketed the business card and gestured towards the door. 'I don't suppose English will wait any more.'

'Don't run,' Verity advised her.

At the end of the Lightwings' garden there was a

dry-stone wall separating them from a long and narrow wooded area. It was a favourite place for Pudding to sit and scan for mice. There was a tarmac path around the perimeter of the wood. From their living room, the Lightwings could occasionally see the head of a dog walker bobbing past, like a football bouncing along the top of their part of the wall. Sometimes Sophie would run round the circuit, but it wasn't really far enough to test her. To stretch herself, she'd complete ten laps.

Four doors down, Mrs Kelly – the oldest person in the neighbourhood – had much the same view. Occasionally, she probably spotted Sophie's head flying past.

Over the next few days, Sophie pounded round the tarmac path, again and again. On sentry, Pudding sometimes watched her dash past. Each time she went by Mrs Kelly's dry-stone wall, she checked that there weren't any dog walkers in view and that Mrs Kelly wasn't looking out of her back windows, before removing a few of the bigger stones from her section of the wall. Sophie threw them a short distance into the wood. After several laps, the dry-stone wall looked severely vandalised.

Mrs Kelly always went to the shops at ten o'clock every Saturday morning. And that's where Sophie bumped into her. The elderly neighbour said, 'Oh. How are you, young … er … ?'

'Sophie.'

'Yes. That's it.'

'I'm fine. Been running round the wood at the back.'

'Good for you.'

'I thought I'd better tell you about your wall.'

'What about it?'

'Well, sorry, but someone's vandalised it.'

'How do you mean?'

'I saw some boys mucking about,' Sophie explained. 'I reckon they thought it'd be fun to pull your wall apart. You know what boys are like. They've taken the stones and thrown them all over the place.'

'I thought it looked … there's a sort of dip in the middle.'

'Yes, that's it. You need someone who'll repair a dry-stone wall.'

Mrs Kelly pulled a face. 'I don't want a man I don't know in my garden.'

'No? You'll have to look out for a woman who'll do it. Would that make a difference? I bet there is one somewhere.'

'Mmm.' Mrs Kelly sounded doubtful. In her day, women didn't build walls.

On the way to training, Sophie wiped her fingerprints off the Lady Gardener's business card and dropped it through Mrs Kelly's letterbox.

'Some boys broke the wall at the bottom of my garden. A real nuisance, I can tell you. But here's a funny thing,' Mrs Kelly announced. 'I talked to someone about it, saying I need a nice lady to put it right. Can't remember who. Anyway, before you know it, a lady gardener puts a small postcard thing through my door.'

Sophie smiled, pleased that her neighbour had such a dreadful memory. She'd forgotten that they'd spoken about the dry-stone wall. 'That's good,' she replied. 'Have you fixed anything up with her?'

'Yes. Seems she'll tackle the job.'

'When's she doing it?'

'This weekend,' Mrs Kelly told her. 'Look. I've written it down to remind me. Saturday afternoon. Two o'clock.'

Sophie nodded. 'It'll be good to have it back in one piece.'

'Yes.'

The repairing of a dry-stone wall provided Sophie with a more realistic opportunity than the driving of a bus. And a large stone made a more realistic weapon than an entire bus. Already, she felt the adrenalin stirring within her body. On Saturday, she would be able to liberate Verity from a toxic mother and achieve a high like no other.

22

Sophie wasn't particularly talented at football but she could run faster and further than anyone else. That made her a real asset for breakaway attacks. The defenders would pump the ball out, always aiming for a spot about ten metres ahead of Sophie's position. She'd run on to it, take it up the wing and cross to any team member in the middle who'd kept up with the pace of play. This time, the striker who didn't quite manage to get her head on the ball was Ursula Graham.

'Come on, Ursula,' Miss Stevens shouted. 'You're not going to get in the England squad like that. Throw yourself at it.'

Walking back down the school pitch with Sophie, Ursula muttered between deep breaths, 'I can think of better things to throw myself at.'

'Like Nathan.'

'Huh.'

Miss Stevens – coach, referee and PE teacher rolled into one – said to them, 'Less natter, more action.'

Once Miss Stevens had blown her whistle and run across the pitch to the site of a foul, Ursula said to Sophie, 'Actually, Mum's playing up over Nathan.'

'Why? He looks ... okay.'

'His looks have got a lot to do with it. She says, "I'm not a racist or anything, but ... " Then she says she doesn't want me going out with him. She only said it after she saw him. Not racist! How stupid does she think I am?'

Sophie set off to chase the lofted free kick. Ursula groaned and made another dash for the penalty area, hoping to shake off her two markers. Sophie's cross didn't reach a good height but it was powerful. It deflected off the hip of one of the opponents, struck Ursula on the chest and went in. Ursula raised her arms and cried, 'Yes!'

A defender muttered, 'If you'd got any sort of bust, that wouldn't have happened.'

Sophie and Ursula had a celebratory hug before walking back to the halfway line. Like sisters, the two girls resembled each other, but it was obvious which was Sophie whenever they broke into a run.

'What excuse did your mum give?' Sophie asked.

'Gangs. Heard bad things about him. I'm aiming too low. "You can do better than someone like this Nathan."

Anything but his skin colour.' She shrugged. 'Where I see a boy, she sees a stereotype.'

'She sounds awful.'

'She's a nut with guns as well.'

'Guns?'

'She's in a shooting club. If a boyfriend puts a foot wrong … '

'You'd better watch out with Nathan.'

'She's ruined Saturday night, that's for sure.'

'Saturday, eh?' Thinking about it, Sophie hesitated. 'Maybe there's something … '

Unable to refuse the challenge of a race, Sophie broke off to pursue a loose ball. It was a hopeless case, but she nearly nicked it from an opponent in midfield.

'That's the sort of enthusiasm I want to see,' Miss Stevens called out.

The match ended in a draw. None of the girls was much concerned with the score, but Miss Stevens kept count and declared it a good, close game.

In the changing rooms, Ursula whispered to Sophie, 'What's on your mind? About Saturday, I mean.'

'How does your mum check on you?'

'She calls my mobile. She's got an app that tells her where I am – or at least where my phone is.'

'That's pretty extreme.'

'Yeah.'

Sophie thought for a moment. 'We could swap phones.'

'How would that work?'

'You tell your mum you're round my house. She'll call your mobile on Saturday night. I'll answer and say something like, "Yes. Ursula's here with me. She's … er … just gone to the loo. Left her phone in the living room." Will that do the job or will she hang on to speak to you?'

'No. She'll take your word for it. I think so anyway.'

'That's all right then. You can be out with Nathan.'

Ursula nodded slowly. 'And what do I do with your phone?'

'Well, there is something. In the afternoon. I'd like to send a text message about three o'clock.'

'Why don't you just do it?'

'You know I did forensic science on my work experience?'

'Yes.'

'They can trace where you are when you send texts. I want to send my dad a message without him knowing where I am. Where will you be in the afternoon?'

'At the shopping mall.'

'Great. I'll write the text and you can press 'send' while you're there. When dad traces the message – he's a policeman – it'll look like I'm in a public place. Well away from mischief.'

'What if he – or anyone else – calls?'

'Don't answer.' Sophie paused before adding, 'I could give you some cash as well and you can buy me some protein powder from the health-food shop. And get a receipt for it.'

Ursula frowned. 'What are you trying to cover up?'

'You want to con your mum. I want to con my dad,' Sophie replied. 'It's just that one of the forensic scientists – Mike – was seriously cute. You know. Dad wouldn't approve because of the age gap. He's quite a bit older than me.'

Ursula seemed unsure. 'Is he all right, though? This Mike. Not a weirdo?'

'More than all right.'

'Are you going to be safe?'

'Sure. I'll give you my phone before you go to the shops and get it back when you've finished. And I'll take yours away so I can field any calls from your mum later on.'

Ursula sighed. 'I'm feeling a bit nervous about it. What if I'm wrong and Mum insists on talking to me?'

Sophie shrugged but maintained her air of confidence. 'I'm sorry, Mrs Graham. Her battery's really low. I'll get her to call you back if there's enough juice, but don't worry if she doesn't. She's fine with me.'

At last, Ursula smiled. 'Okay. We'll do each other a favour.'

'It's a deal.'

23

Sophie was desperate to feel rapture once more. She'd do anything to experience it again. Having sampled it, she knew she couldn't go on without savouring it time after time. Already, she was addicted to it. The elation that swept over her when blood flowed was becoming her reason for living.

If a few people had to die for her fulfilment, that's just the way it had to be. It was a small price to pay for such enjoyment and she chose horrible people anyway.

She wasn't the only one who benefited either. Freed from stifling relationships, her friends did too.

She used to think that running was everything, but now she knew that, if some terrible accident ruined her legs, she'd be able to carry on without the thrill of racing. But if someone or something stopped her achieving that other thrill, the ultimate thrill, she would have no reason to continue.

'I'm off into town,' she announced to her parents after lunch on Saturday. 'All right?'

'Take care, love.'

'Will do.'

Of course, she didn't head for the shopping mall. Instead, she sought ecstasy. She pulled on her gloves, checked the time and went for a run at the club before returning to the wood. She approached the back of Mrs Kelly's house warily, keeping her head down so that she was invisible to any neighbours looking out from their windows. The wood was quiet. No barking, no shouting.

Almost exactly three o'clock. As she crept towards the broken wall, though, she heard regular clunks of heavy stones being lifted, stacked and adjusted. The noise was even louder than the thudding of her own heart. Verity's mother was working entirely within Mrs Kelly's garden. Clearly, the gardener had already gathered up the stones scattered in the wood and piled them on Mrs Kelly's lawn. Except for the one that Sophie had concealed behind a tree that morning.

Denise Wilson had raised the level of the wall and was beginning to organise the topping stones, roughly triangular in shape. Nearing the spot unseen, an excited Sophie smiled broadly. It was perfect. Mrs Wilson had built up enough height to hide Sophie.

She glanced around. Still no dog walkers. Still keeping her head down. Still perfect. Making sure she would be out of Mrs Kelly's sight if she was gazing out of her back window, Sophie appeared suddenly opposite Verity's mum and said, 'Hello.'

Mrs Wilson jumped in shock and dropped a stone. 'Oh. It's you. Sophie Lightwing.'

'Sorry,' Sophie said. 'I didn't mean to scare you.'

Denise muttered something under her breath.

This, Sophie thought, was going to be divine. 'I'm just trying to be helpful,' she said. 'I can see a stone you missed. Do you want it? I think it's one of the big ones that go on top.'

'All right,' the Lady Gardener replied, with no hint of gratitude.

Sophie walked a few paces and then lifted the stone in her gloved right hand. It was a perfect weight and shape. Triangular. At once, she could hear Ranji Nawaz's voice in her head. '*This side's for thoughts. This one here is for feelings and the third one's for behaviour. Because that's how it works, isn't it? We think about something. The thought makes us feel happy, sad or whatever. And that affects what we do. What we're feeling makes us behave in a certain way.*' Sophie was thinking about killing and doing Verity a favour. She was feeling absolutely great. And that affected what she was about to do. Pleasure drove her behaviour.

Relishing the moment, another image came to Sophie's mind. Another almost triangular object. An iron.

Flat base, pointed top. Sophie grabbed the stone along its flat base, leaving the jagged apex protruding. That's what would do the damage.

Looking left and right along the deserted path, she went back to where Verity's mother was working. 'Here it is,' she said. 'Ready?'

'Just give it to me.'

'Sure will.'

Still not lifting her head above the wall, Sophie lunged forward with her arm and hurled the stone, surprising the Lady Gardener. The pointed end crashed into her forehead and blood welled up instantly around the stone.

Sophie gasped in delight. She leapt to one side, but the spurt of red liquid splashed against the other side of the wall, protecting her from any staining. At once, Mrs Wilson dropped out of sight. That was a disappointment, of course, but it was inevitable.

Working quickly and ignoring Pudding, who was padding along the wall towards her, Sophie picked up a branch with a flattened end. She jammed it into a crevice in the newly built wall and heaved downwards with all her strength. The makeshift lever lifted up the top layers of stone until they toppled inwards towards Mrs Kelly's lawn. Even though Sophie couldn't see because she was keeping low and out of sight, she knew the stones would have clattered down on Verity's mum. She could summon the beautiful image in her mind: the incompetent Lady

Gardener hadn't made the structure stable enough. She'd caused her own death by doing a shoddy job.

Still holding the branch, Sophie ran along the path, almost skipping with joy. Well away from the collapsed wall, she jettisoned the pretend crowbar, launching it like a javelin into the wood.

Sophie felt she did not have to concern herself with the rights and wrongs of her actions. For her, there was only necessity.

24

'Yes, I'll tell you what happened,' Mrs Kelly said to the police officer in her back room. 'I saw it all. A stone just came out of nowhere. I think it fell off the wall. It must have done. Anyway, it hit her. She keeled over. Then the wall she'd been putting up wobbled and crashed down on her. The whole lot. It was terrible. Dreadful.'

Sergeant Yorke asked, 'And you saw all this with your own eyes?'

'Yes. I was sitting where you are now, looking out.'

Sergeant Yorke twisted towards the window. He was a little low, but he had a good view of the area that was now segregated with yellow tape. His colleagues were combing the site, paying particular attention to the gardener's body. 'Did you see anyone else around at the time?'

'Anyone else? No. It was just the Lady Gardener.' Mrs Kelly hesitated.

'Are you sure?'

'There was a cat walking along the wall. That's all.'

'Did you call 999 straightaway?'

'Well, I went down to see if she was all right first.'

'Did you touch anything or move anything?'

'No.' Mrs Kelly shuddered. 'I just called out but … you know. She didn't … It was a horrible sight.'

Sergeant Yorke scribbled a few notes and then stood up.

Still visibly shaken, Mrs Kelly said, 'I'm not in trouble for getting her to do the job, am I?'

The officer smiled sympathetically. 'No. Don't worry. It was her choice to take it on. We'll have to look into whether she was qualified to do it, though.'

Coffee in hand, DI Zena Kirkland said, 'Well, it's happened again.'

'What has?' Sergeant Lightwing replied.

'That accident just along the road from you. The victim's daughter is friendly with your Sophie.'

Tony looked puzzled. 'You said it yourself. An accident. You've even got an eyewitness who says so. I know Mrs Kelly. Doddery but reliable.'

'But something else is niggling me now, Tony.'

'Oh?'

'You see, the wall collapsed on her. All her wounds are consistent with that – with an accident – except for the fatal one. If, say, she tripped, clutched at the unfinished wall and it gave way, she'd fall. If she landed on her back, the stones would have dropped on her from a metre and a half. Two at most. But the one that killed her landed with more force than gravity can account for. Odd, don't you think? It was like it hit her forehead from a height of about four or five metres. Or someone walloped her with it.'

'Maybe she fell onto the stone, not the other way round. That'd generate a lot of force.'

'She would've landed on her front in that case. She was face-up.'

Tony shrugged.

'I'm going to have to interview Sophie.'

'Hold on. What time did it happen?'

'The emergency call came in at 3.09, to be precise. Death was just before.'

'Sophie was out shopping. Miles away.'

'I'll ask her to prove that.'

Tony laughed. A nervous laugh, though. 'You don't have to. She sent me a text. It was the same time.' He held out his phone. 'See. Two minutes past three. You've got my permission to triangulate and find out where she was at the time. You'll find it was the shopping mall. And when you do,' Sergeant Lightwing said, 'I'd like to hear you explain how she got from the town centre to nearly home in zero time. She's fast, but she's not Superman. Superwoman, I mean.'

'We'll see.'

'She also bought some stuff. She told me. If she's got the receipt … '

'Yes. I'd like to see that.'

'A receipt?' Sophie said to her dad. 'Yes. Well, no. I don't know. I put it in the bin.'

'Which bin?' Tony asked.

'Kitchen, I think. Why?'

'Oh, it doesn't matter. Just a way of telling everyone where you were on Saturday afternoon.'

Sophie shrugged.

With a frown, her father delved into the bin. After a minute of rummaging among the waste, he emerged triumphantly with a tea-stained, screwed-up receipt. 'Still just about legible,' he said to himself as he spread it out and sealed it in a small, transparent bag. First thing the next morning, he'd hand it over to Zena Kirkland.

The manager of the health-food shop directed Sergeant Yorke to the assistant at the pay-point. 'I'm told,' the police officer said to him, 'you were serving on Saturday afternoon.'

At once cautious, he answered, 'That's right.'

'Do you remember anyone buying protein powder?'

'Vile stuff, but popular with bodybuilders. I probably sold a few packs.'

'All to bodybuilders?'

He shrugged. 'Do you know how many people come in here on a Saturday? It was very busy.'

The police officer scanned the ceiling and walls before asking, 'Do you have a security camera covering where we are? The queue for the till.'

'No. Only the back shelves that you can't see from here.'

'Is that where the protein powder is, by any chance?'

'No. It's behind you. There.'

'Out of camera shot.'

'Yes.'

Sergeant Yorke showed the shop assistant Sophie's receipt. 'Just before three o'clock, it says.'

The shop assistant examined the dishevelled piece of paper inside its protective bag. 'Yes, this was me. My code at the bottom. But I don't remember who bought it.'

Sergeant Yorke held out a photo of Sophie Lightwing. 'How about her? Did she come into the shop?'

Stroking his chin, the assistant replied, 'Maybe. There was a girl like her, I think. She could've been the one, I suppose.'

'But you're not sure.'

'Not certain, no. But, now you mention it, I remember thinking she didn't look like a bodybuilder.'

'Okay. Thanks.'

Before leaving the shopping mall, Sergeant Yorke visited Security at DI Kirkland's request and commandeered all of their CCTV footage from Saturday afternoon.

In her office, Dr Ranji Nawaz shook her head. 'I don't know where you got your information from, but Sophie Lightwing's not my patient any more.'

Detective Inspector Zena Kirkland replied, 'But she used to be.'

'Yes.'

'And I assume you still have her best interests at heart.'

'Of course. I also have patient confidentiality at heart.'

The police officer smiled. 'I wouldn't dream of putting you in an awkward position. I just want to ask a theoretical question. That's all.'

Suspicious, Ranji waited.

'You're an expert in brain disorders.'

'Memory, mainly.'

'In your opinion, if mothers known to a certain girl started to die in mysterious circumstances – mostly blows to the head – do you think I ought to concern myself with that girl? Especially if she'd witnessed her own mother's death by repeated blows to the head.'

Trying not to show her alarm, Ranji said, 'I can't

possibly answer that. It's so thinly disguised, it's obviously a question about one of my ex-patients.'

'I'm not asking you to divulge anything specific about any particular patient,' DI Kirkland replied. 'I'm just seeking your professional opinion. If there were such a girl, is there any reason she should figure in my inquiries?'

'You're fishing around and I'm not having it. I suggest you speak to Professor Dench, a brain researcher at the university. Perhaps he'll be willing to shed a little light on the matter.'

Zena made sure that she encountered Sergeant Lightwing – apparently by chance – at HQ. 'Ah, Tony,' she said. 'Something odd's just cropped up again. We've looked at every frame of every camera in the shopping mall on Saturday and we can't spot your Sophie anywhere around three o'clock. A few girls like her, but no sign of Sophie.'

'That doesn't mean she wasn't there. She must have been. The text and the receipt prove it,' Tony replied. 'Presumably she didn't wander in front of any CCTV. Or maybe you didn't get the angle that showed her face.'

DI Kirkland nodded. 'Maybe that's it. I'll keep you informed.'

With obvious pride, Professor Dench explained to Zena Kirkland his method for softening disturbing memories. 'It's a big step forward. Hard to appreciate how significant it is until you've seen someone crippled with severe trauma or a phobia. The turn-around is phenomenal. A boy who loathed buttons now takes great delight in collecting and organising them. A woman with an extreme fear of spiders now keeps them as pets and a man petrified of heights goes rock climbing.'

'I'm not here for spiders, buttons and heights. I'm in a very different league.'

'I don't see what any of it has got to do with the law.'

'It does if it endangers people's lives.'

'What do you mean? What's happened?'

Zena kept quiet about her enquiries, like a medic steering away from confidential details on a patient. Ignoring his question, she said, 'I'm not an expert, but it seems to me you're on the edge of a boundary. Helping people to cope with painful memories and phobias is one thing. Fiddling with their brains until they enjoy whatever used to haunt them is way over the line. Surely. Is Sophie Lightwing one of your patients?'

'Yes, but … '

Interrupting, Zena didn't give him the opportunity to mention confidentiality. 'If you treat a girl for trauma after she's seen her mother murdered, will she develop a taste for similar deaths? Like buttons? Like spiders and heights? Is that what you're telling me?'

Professor Dench's mood changed abruptly. 'My method doesn't aim to go that far. That's no more than a theoretical possibility.'

'But it *is* a possibility.'

The professor shrugged. 'Theoretically. Even if it *did* happen, in the case of bloodshed, I'd expect morality to outweigh any over-compensation by the brain treatment. That would inhibit any violent behaviour.'

'That's theoretical as well.'

'We haven't completed a full clinical trial yet. But all my work has proper approval.'

'Do you monitor your patients afterwards?' Zena asked.

'Of course. Until we're sure they're a success. Until they're capable of a normal life.'

'No long-term monitoring?'

'I don't have the funds for that.'

25

Overflowing with lactic acid, her legs were like lead weights. Even her arms felt heavy and her lungs were on fire. She blew out the carbon dioxide and gasped down fresh air, fresh oxygen. Sophie's brain sent out an urgent message for yet more effort from her jaded legs. But there was no response. There was no enthusiasm for more pain. She was exhausted. The only runners in front of her were a few men, twice her age. All of the other competitors were behind her as she neared the finishing arch with *Yorkshire Park 5km* written across the top. The clock showed 17:20.

Alluring images of Carmen Hope, Florence Quinn and Denise Wilson – senseless before death – came to her mind, providing welcome relief. The distraction overpowered all feelings of pain. She gave up coaxing every last drop of physical energy from her body because her brain provided complete mental satisfaction.

Jonah had somehow summoned up a sprint finish. He was closing fast on Sophie and on a personal best. In the crowd, his uncle was shouting encouragement.

There would be no personal best for Sophie. Not this time. Even so, her mum and dad were cheering like crazy.

Their coach was scowling as always, concentrating on what Sophie and Jonah could do better, rather than celebrating their achievement. The other spectators clapped and called out their approval of the battle between the two young runners. Then, suddenly, it was all over. They crossed the line together.

'Who won?'

'Did he catch her up?'

'Not sure.'

'Dead heat, I think.'

Side-by-side, Sophie and Jonah stopped, bent over, hands on hips, and took great mouthfuls of air. Sweat ran down their faces and backs. An official handed them each a bottle of water and someone else gave both of them a medal and a winner's T-shirt. They nodded their thanks then looked at each other. Two shattered grimaces. But Sophie saw an edge behind Jonah's expression and it was nothing to do with the race.

At last, a voice thundered, 'That was too close to call, ladies and gentlemen! Let's hear it for them. First female runner home – Sophie Lightwing. First junior male runner: Jonah Quinn. And the chip timing tells me that winner of the junior race – by a tenth of a second – was … ' The steward's amplified voice waited an age before finishing the announcement. 'Sophie Lightwing.'

There wasn't a formal podium presentation, but in the park there was genuine appreciation of both performances.

More competitors flashed past on their way to the huge inflatable arch but, after taking the congratulations of their families, Sophie and Jonah were lying down on the grass together, taking a few moments to assess and appreciate what they'd done.

With that strange look on his face again, Jonah turned towards his friend and rival. 'I've figured out how you did it.'

'By being faster?'

'I wasn't talking about that.'

'What then?' Sophie asked.

'You saw where I left my key when I went on the school trip, didn't you? You could have taken it. And there's the alarm, but you saw me put the code in. You were behind me that time. I bet you still know it.'

Sophie shook her head.

'I showed you the spreadsheet as well. You knew when Mum would be home and Dad still at work. That's all you needed. You killed her. Well, no, you didn't. Not really you. Something not right in your head did it.'

'Me? You're kidding. The police know who did it.'

'They're wrong.'

'Really?'

'I went to see Dad. He still says he didn't do it.' Jonah wiped his face with his hand. 'I believe him.'

'But … '

'What?'

'You've come out of it really well. Your uncle's here, supporting you.'

Jonah took a deep breath. 'Dad's going to go to prison for years for something he didn't do. He might be a bigot but he doesn't deserve that.'

'So what are you going to do with your theory? Tell the police?'

'No.' Jonah stood up. Almost in tears, he said, 'I'll leave that to you. It's your responsibility. *You* tell them.'

Even before Jonah was out of sight, Sophie could see Ranji Nawaz approaching. 'Ah, there you are,' the doctor said to her former patient. 'I was just having a walk. I didn't know there was a race on.'

Lie, Sophie thought.

'As soon as I realised,' Ranji continued, 'I guessed you'd be in it, so I stayed to watch.' She sprawled on the grass and asked, 'How are you doing?'

'I'm fine. Could have run better. That's all.'

'You looked good to me. I saw you finish. Junior winner. Impressive.'

Sophie took a gulp of water. 'I'm normally way in front of Jonah.'

Ranji nodded. 'Maybe your mind wasn't fully engaged.'

'You always used to blame my brain – for anything and everything. But it's fixed now.'

'When we've got other things on our mind – important things – it has an effect on what we're doing. Have you ever tried to listen to music while you're taking a phone call? We're easily distracted.' Ranji waved away a fly and turned her head towards Sophie. 'So, the question is: what else is on your mind? Has something become more important to you than running?'

'No.'

'Let me show you something.' Ranji fiddled with her phone and then held it out so they could both watch a YouTube video. A short clip of an over-confident woman on a treadmill in a gym. The runner turned up the speed to impress everyone with her fitness. But she couldn't keep up with the running machine and her legs slipped backwards. Her head went forwards and smacked heavily on the touchscreen.

At the moment of impact – the woman's head striking the control panel – Ranji gazed at her ex-patient and saw an immediate wicked glint in her eyes. Ranji saw far more pleasure on Sophie's face than the woman's pratfall deserved. The normal human reaction was a wince followed by humour. Sophie didn't wince.

She skipped the sympathy and went directly to enjoyment.

Straightaway, Ranji guessed what the reprogramming of Sophie's brain had done.

Looking away from the screen, Sophie jumped up and – without a word – strode towards her parents. 'I want to go home now,' she announced.

'Oh. Okay,' her mum said. 'Let's go.'

26

Like that familiar scene in an ancient horror film, walls were closing in on Sophie. That's certainly how she felt. Jonah, Ranji Nawaz, and some detective who'd asked her dad to find that receipt: they were all pressing in on her, ganging up on her, trying to stop her achieving those highs again. Highs that she *had* to have.

So far, she'd had the luxury of taking her time. She'd been able to calculate each kill calmly and carefully. Now, with those walls moving in, cramping her style, she had to act fast, take risks, or be denied what she craved most. Maybe Mrs Graham – with her love of guns – had appeared on Sophie's radar at the perfect time.

On Sophie's lap, the contented purring ceased as soon as her hand stopped its automatic stroking. Abruptly, she stood and Pudding leapt to the safety of the carpet. 'Sorry,' Sophie said to the cat. 'Things to do.'

Emily Graham opened the door, looked at her visitor and announced, 'She's not here.'

'Oh,' Sophie said, as if she were disappointed that Ursula wasn't at home. 'She texted to say she'd meet me here. Is it okay if I come in and wait?'

Ursula's mother sighed. 'I suppose.' She stood to one side.

'Thanks.'

As they went into the living room, Emily asked, 'Did she say who she was with?'

Sophie shrugged. 'Not exactly. Some of the girls. That's all.'

Mrs Graham's middle-aged skin was tight across her forehead. Ripe for cracking. 'She didn't mention a boy?'

'No.' Sophie strolled towards a glass-fronted cabinet, crammed with medals and cups. The illustrated ones showed a person aiming a rifle. 'Oh, yes, you're into shooting, aren't you? Ursula told me.'

Mrs Graham nodded. 'I've got a Firearm Certificate, yes.'

Sophie got the impression that Ursula's mum was eager to share her favourite hobby, but she was reluctant to chat to a youngster about it. To loosen her up, Sophie said, 'You know my dad's a police officer? He wants me to get into guns, but … ' She shrugged.

'That's all right, then. A policeman's daughter.

I could give you a taster right now, if you want. As long as your dad would approve.'

'Yes, he would but, no, I don't … Well, maybe. At least I'd know what to say when he lectures me about it again.'

'They're locked away. They have to be – by law.' Mrs Graham grasped a keyring attached to her belt, selected one of the two keys and went to a large safe attached to the far wall. Fiddling with the lock, she said, 'I'm always cautious about who I show rifles to, but it's different with you, being a policeman's daughter.' She opened the door, revealing three large firearms positioned on racks.

'They're huge,' said Sophie.

Extracting one of the rifles, Emily asked, 'What did you expect?'

'Well, you know. Something small. You couldn't walk down the street, whip one of those out of your pocket and surprise someone.'

Ursula's mum smiled. 'You've been watching too many films. Especially American ones. Handguns are illegal here. Precisely to stop bad guys whipping them out of their pockets and surprising someone. Mine are all rifles. Perfectly legal. Do you want to hold this one?'

'No, not … Oh, all right. I'll give it a go.' Sophie slipped her sports bag off her shoulder and dropped it on to an armchair.

Mrs Graham showed her how to grip the weapon. 'Point two two. Semi-automatic. My favourite.'

'They're terrible really,' Sophie said, 'but, standing like this, it makes you feel … powerful. Awesome.'

Emily agreed. 'They definitely give you a buzz.'

'When you're aiming at a target or whatever, do you ever think of people you don't like?'

Mrs Graham looked askance at Sophie. 'No. It's a target, that's all. An exercise.'

'Not even a tiny bit?'

'No.'

'Not even Nathan?'

'That's enough.'

Sophie asked, 'Is it loaded?'

Mrs Graham laughed uneasily. 'No. Otherwise, I wouldn't have let you have it.'

'How do you load it, though?'

Ursula's mum held out her hand for the weapon. 'I'm not going that far. For obvious reasons. We don't want any accidents, do we?'

Sophie kept hold of the rifle. 'Definitely not,' she replied, as if appalled by the idea. 'But I bet it's on YouTube anyway.'

'Probably. Anyway, I keep ammunition separate. For safety.'

'The thing is … ' Quickly, Sophie turned and took a savage swipe with the hefty weapon, the butt delivering a delicious clout to Mrs Graham's forehead. With Emily on the floor, stunned, Sophie continued to talk to her as if she could still hear. 'I can guess. You see, you've got two keys here. One for the guns and the other will be for the bullets. So all I need to do is find another locked cupboard. And I did look up loading on the internet before I came. I looked up firing as well. Doesn't make me an expert but … it's enough.'

Shivering with pleasure, Sophie squatted down next to the unconscious woman. She unbuckled her belt and slid off the keyring. Then she went hunting.

She found a safe at the bottom of Mrs Graham's wardrobe. The second key fitted and Sophie opened the heavy door. As she suspected, there were several loaded magazines and boxes of ammunition stacked inside. Remembering the videos she'd watched earlier, she selected one of the magazines. Sitting on the floor, she pointed the gun away from her and shoved the magazine into the underside of the rifle, just forward of the trigger. It snapped into place with a satisfying click. She pulled back the bolt on the side of the gun and let it spring forward again. That meant the first round was in the chamber, ready to fire. Except that it wouldn't. Sophie had done her homework. She knew that the rifle would have its safety catch engaged. She examined the area around the trigger and spotted the mechanism. She pushed and pulled till it moved aside.

Now, the rifle was ready. According to online videos, a simple squeeze of the trigger would do it. The bullet would fly from the gun, the spent cartridge would leap out, and the next round would load into the chamber. All Sophie needed was a trial shot. That's where Mrs Graham figured in her plans. She went back into the living room.

Ursula's mum had crawled across the carpet, leaving a trail of small crimson spots, and hauled herself onto a chair. She was trying to make sense of her phone.

Sophie stood four paces away from her, legs apart for stability. Her adrenalin level surged as she tried to grip the rifle comfortably and took aim. 'Put the phone down,' she demanded.

Emily obeyed. In a faltering voice, as loud as she could manage, she said, 'You put the gun down, Sophie Lightwing.'

Sophie wasn't bothered that Ursula's mum was still trying to continue a call, but she walked up to the phone and ended it. 'That's enough,' she muttered. She breathed deeply twice and shouldered the weapon again. Much closer to her target now, she peered through the rear sight to the front sight and beyond to Mrs Graham. She felt powerful. Awesome. Steeling herself, she said, 'This is for Ursula and Nathan.' But really what she was about to do was for herself. For pure joy.

Slowly, she pulled the trigger. She was ready for the recoil. She knew from YouTube clips that, when she fired, the rifle would kick.

'No, you can't! You're not even holding it prop … '

The bang and the bullet silenced Mrs Graham at once. It didn't enter her where Sophie expected. The jolt of the rifle spoiled her aim. But it was good enough. After all, Ursula's mum was only a means to an end.

Quickly, Sophie engaged the safety mechanism and slid the rifle, stock first, into her sports bag. She hoped that the metal tube poking out would not look like the barrel of a rifle. Anyway, no one would believe that a teenage girl was carrying a gun.

Feeling light-headed, she left for her grand finale.

27

'You asked me,' Ranji Nawaz said into the phone, 'for advice about a theoretical girl who'd watched her mother being murdered.'

'Yes, I did,' DI Kirkland replied.

'You asked if you should concern yourself with her if her friends' mothers died through blows to the head.'

'Yes?' the SIO prompted.

'Did you speak to Professor Dench?'

'Yes.'

'So, you know his method.'

'I know that people who hate spiders can be made to love them.'

'I'm worried,' Ranji said, 'that people who were traumatised by a crime might be made to love the same crime. I'm worried that it might become an addiction – like the worst sort of drug.'

'Thank you.'

'For the sake of everyone – especially that theoretical girl – you ought to be concerned.'

'Well, I can't detain anyone without good evidence, but I appreciate your advice. Very much. Thanks again.'

'Boss. We've got a report of a possible gunshot at a house,' said Sergeant Yorke. 'A neighbour called. I've checked. There's a Firearm Certificate issued to an Emily Graham at the address.'

'Emily Graham?' DI Kirkland typed the name into her computer.

'A couple of uniforms are in the vicinity. Shall I . . . ?'

'We might have a casualty so, yes, get them to nose around outside – with extreme caution. Maybe they'll be able to see what's going on inside. Then they wait for the armed response unit.'

Sergeant Yorke hesitated. 'Hang on. I've got an abandoned emergency call from the same house now. It didn't make any sense, but you can hear a female voice telling Sophie Lightwing to put the gun down.'

'What?' But Zena didn't need a repeat. She typed furiously, fishing around in databases. Then she jumped up. 'Okay. Emily Graham's daughter goes to the same school as Sophie. It's making perfect sense.' She grabbed her coat and then paused to announce to everyone, 'All this is embargoed. It doesn't leave the room. Okay?

I don't want Tony Lightwing in the loop. For his own sake as well as ours.'

28

Sophie strode into the gym of her sports club. She stopped near the main door, squatted beside her bag, extracted the rifle and quickly released the safety catch. Engrossed with their workouts, none of the members noticed. Immediately, Sophie got their attention with a shot fired haphazardly into the ceiling. Two people fell from treadmills and another screamed. A dumbbell crashed onto the floor and an athlete froze in a rowing machine as if becalmed at sea. The whirring of equipment hushed and dangling ropes swayed in the air for a few seconds before coming to a halt. The place lapsed into deathly quiet and stillness.

'Right,' she said, walking further into the room but making sure she had the exit covered. 'Men and kids over there.' She waved the weapon towards the boxing ring. 'Women by the treadmills.' She nodded in the other direction.

‘But … ’

‘What’s … ?’

Mostly, the members moved sheepishly as they were told. A few didn’t seem capable of moving at all. One woman put both hands to the sides of her distressed face. She reminded Sophie of the pained figure in Munch’s painting of a scream.

A young woman with bright red hair spluttered, ‘What about me? I’m eighteen.’

Sophie snorted impatiently. ‘Have you got kids?’

‘Er … yes.’

Sophie smiled. The teenager was lying. She must have thought that Sophie would spare anyone who was a mother. ‘Okay. Let’s make it simple. Mothers by the walking machines. Everyone else over there.’

Three stunned, frightened faces peered into the gym through the glass of the door. Two disappeared straightaway but the other remained transfixed. She did not dare to enter, though. Sophie ignored the girl but, just for a moment, she was eight years old again and she was staring in horror through a narrow gap in a door.

Dispelling the flashback, a familiar woman appeared in front of Sophie. It was the weekend warrior she’d last seen in a bloodied bandana. Now the woman was sweating like a boxer. ‘What’s this?’ she cried. ‘What are you doing? You’re a nice girl. You helped me. Remember?’

Sophie nodded. ‘You split your head open. It felt great.’

'What?'

'Are you a mother?'

'Yes. What's that got to do with it?'

'Move. Join the others.'

'You must know you won't get away with this. Whatever you're doing. You're probably on CCTV. Someone'll be phoning.'

Sophie shot her from the hip.

The weekend warrior twisted unnaturally as the bullet hit. Probably a superficial injury to her shoulder. Not much more than a scratch.

'Move.'

Wincing and clutching her left shoulder, she made for the treadmills and joined eight more women.

Sophie admitted to herself that she was not a good shot. If she was going to do this thing, she would have to get closer to each victim. 'All in a line, on your knees,' she ordered the mothers. 'You first,' she said to the weekend warrior.

29

The team was satisfied that the house was secure. Medics were treating Emily Graham's wounds, which weren't life-threatening. Two constables were trying to trace Ursula's whereabouts. The armed officers were checking the remaining rifles against Emily Graham's licence, confirming that the weapon used against her was no longer at the crime scene. If Sophie Lightwing was the culprit – and there was little doubt in Zena Kirkland's mind – she was on the loose with a self-loading point two two calibre rifle.

'I've got a disturbance at the sports club just down the road now,' Sergeant Yorke said to his SIO. 'Not sure what's happening, but someone says there's a girl with a gun. Three separate reports of two shots being fired. And a good number of hostages.'

'Lightwing runs at that club,' Zena said. 'Decamp

from here. I want an all-male team. Okay? Apart from me. Women are going to be targets. They stay here. The rest of us are on our way.'

Sirens squealing, eight police cars converged on the sports centre and quarantined the main building. Armed officers crouched behind cars and two more were making for the rooftop of the building opposite. DI Kirkland ran the whole show from one particular car. Barking out orders, she told someone to get hold of Ranji Nawaz from the Institute for Memory Disorders. Zena was not going to be tempted into hasty action. She might value the doctor's advice, but what she needed most was information and communication from inside the club.

When she next looked towards the sports centre, she let out a shriek. 'Who's that?'

A young man had simply walked brazenly through the cordon.

'Who let that boy through?' she yelled.

'Shall I go after him?' asked Sergeant Yorke.

DI Kirkland sighed and shook her head. 'Too late. He doesn't know what he's getting into.'

30

For a moment, Sophie listened to the sirens and smiled. She knew the odds were stacked against her, but she didn't mind. She would get satisfaction one way or another. If she started shooting, she would experience supreme bliss until the police rushed in and overwhelmed her. If she did nothing but threaten a bloodbath, the police would have no option but to eliminate the danger before anyone was killed. She hoped for a head-shot. When the marksman's bullet struck her, she expected to experience the ultimate high. There would be two different explosions. She expected the first – the irresistible chemical explosion of endorphins and oxytocin – to bring unimaginable delight before the second – the physical explosion – devastated her brain. Such intense ecstasy would be a fitting end. After that, any further life would be unnecessary, a disappointment.

She looked down again at the injured weekend warrior. The first in a neat row of kneeling mothers, lined up like ducks in a fairground shooting gallery. Out of the corner of her eye, though, Sophie saw the door opening. Turning towards it, she expected to see a trained marksman. She expected to offer herself for the final thrill. But it wasn't a police officer at all. It was a familiar friend. In the silence of the gym, she stepped back and said, 'Are you stalking me again, Jonah Quinn?'

Jonah nodded. 'Yes. I know what this is all about now.' He walked towards her, trying to position himself between her and the line of whimpering mothers.

Sophie pointed the rifle at him. 'Don't get in my way.'

'Don't do this.'

'Why not?'

'It's not you, Sophie. It's not what you are.'

'Isn't it?'

'I don't blame you for my mum. I never will. You're not well.' He glanced around the gym. 'All this proves it. Whatever's gnawing away in your brain is what's to blame.'

'I'm warning you.'

'When I came in, you looked disappointed. Just for a second.'

'So?'

'There's enough police out there to win a war. You want them to shoot you.'

'So, you're a brain expert now.'

'When I said you should tell the police, I didn't mean to announce yourself like this. I meant something like a talk with your dad.'

'I'm not into confessing. This is what I want,' Sophie insisted, indicating the rifle. 'This is how it's got to be. It's my moment.'

Jonah shook his head. 'You know why I'm stalking you? It's not for my dad – who didn't kill anyone. It's not even for them.' He waved towards the mothers, awaiting their execution.

'Oh?'

'You're not going to kill them. You're just provoking a reaction.'

'So who are you here for?'

'You know perfectly well. I'm here for you, Sophie. Because I like you. Very much. But something's gone wrong up here.' Jonah tapped the side of his head. 'Someone can fix it. Someone can sort you out. And give me my running mate back.'

'I don't want to shoot you.'

'You don't have to. You don't have to shoot anyone.'

'You don't understand. Someone's got to be shot.'

On the far side of the hall, some of the men were quietly ushering children towards a fire door. Sophie knew, but she didn't care. As far as she was concerned, they could all go. Only Jonah stood between her and an immense prize.

'You're right,' he said. 'I don't understand. But I know it's wrong.'

'What are you going to do about it?'

'I'm going to do you a favour.'

Sophie frowned. 'How do you mean?'

Jonah's head dropped and he sighed. Then, suddenly, he threw himself forward, directly at Sophie, hoping to knock her over and disarm her before she could pull the trigger.

But he wasn't fast enough.

Taken by surprise, Sophie fired. She wasn't sure if she meant to shoot Jonah. Maybe she did. Maybe his lurch merely nudged her finger on the trigger. But it was done. She couldn't undo it.

As he fell back, Jonah grabbed the barrel of the rifle and yanked it away from Sophie's grasp. Another round discharged. There was a ruby splash on the right side of his head as the bullet whistled past his ear.

He couldn't hold on to the weapon. His flailing arm flung it across the gym.

One of the mothers jumped up immediately and raced towards the rifle. She picked it up, stared at Sophie and took aim. 'Don't even think about it. I'm a member of the rifle club. I know exactly what to do.'

Sophie wasn't interested. She gazed at Jonah and muttered, 'I'm really sorry, Jonah. You shouldn't have … '

The woman with the rifle snapped the safety catch into place, removed the magazine and pulled back the bolt to empty the barrel of its live round. 'It's safe,' she shouted to the others. 'Come on!' Holding the disabled firearm, she made for the exit.

Blood was trickling from Jonah's ear. Still on his feet, but unsteady with shock, he lifted up his left arm. Looking down, he saw a ragged hole through his sweatshirt, glistening red. But he was upright. He was alive. The bullet had passed between his torso and his arm, only grazing his body.

He staggered back and stared in surprise at Sophie. 'You missed!'

Sophie was pleased and disappointed at the same time. She hadn't killed her friend, but she had been denied heaven. Defeated, her smile was weak and wretched. 'I'm a terrible shot,' she said.

Part 2

PUNISHMENT

31

Everything about the room was grey. There was an empty table, a few chairs, bland walls, a single door, some sort of recording device and little else. Sophie sat and waited for something to happen, missing Pudding and any sort of human contact. She longed to be pounding around a track. Restless, she stood and went through some squatting and jumping exercises instead. But she had no enthusiasm for a workout. She sat down again.

She was in legal limbo: that place between arrest and either release or prosecution. For Sophie, it was a place that led to heaven or to hell. Her actions in the interview room would decide her fate. Until some official sent her plunging down through a trapdoor, she was tempted to strive for that other exit, for more running, more adrenalin, more killing.

Looking exasperated, Sergeant Lightwing burst into the room. 'Sophie.'

'Dad.'

He hugged her for a moment and then pulled away, leaving his hands on her shoulders. 'I've only got a couple of minutes.'

'Okay.'

'What's going on? Why did you … ?'

'They were my friends. I had to help them out. Had to.'

Her father's face creased with puzzlement. 'What are we talking about?'

'Beth, Jonah and Verity Wilson.'

Tony Lightwing's arms fell to his sides. 'Are you saying … ? I was only talking about this rifle thing.'

'Killing's like running, Dad. Only more intense. Scary, but definitely exciting. I had no choice. It made me feel alive.'

Mouth open, Tony looked devastated. Utterly broken. It was the expression of someone dealt a fatal blow but yet to fall. An expression that was now familiar to Sophie. Her father shook his head, trying to come to his senses. 'Look. They'll question you. Any moment. Don't say what you've just said to me. Don't admit to anything. All right? It's really important. Vital. Say absolutely nothing. You'll get a duty solicitor. She'll advise you, but don't say anything that's remotely a confession. Okay? Zena – DI Kirkland – is making a limited disclosure to the solicitor right now, briefing her on the case. She'll fill you in.'

Sophie nodded. 'No confession.'

'That's right.' He glanced at his watch. 'I've got to go. I shouldn't really be here.' He gave her a final tentative hug. 'What will your mum … ?' He sighed hopelessly. 'Oh, Sophie.'

Sophie smiled at him. 'You and Mum wanted me fixed. You wanted me like this.'

Tony's face crumpled even further. 'No. Not this.'

32

DI Kirkland sat opposite Sophie and introduced everyone like an over-fussy host at a very dull party. She also announced the time and date. The detective's painted eyebrows lurched upwards and then arched back down, making her look perpetually surprised. By her side, a younger male colleague sat in silence with a penetrating stare cemented onto his face.

Sophie's solicitor sat alongside her. She looked relaxed, alert and confident. Leaning on the wall to Sophie's left, the responsible adult stood, gazing at the suspect with a carefully neutral expression. Sophie didn't understand what he was there for, but she liked the idea of a responsible adult. He was responsible and she wasn't.

The setup didn't trouble Sophie. She seemed to have spent a lifetime sitting in a room with adults who quizzed her incessantly.

Zena Kirkland eased back in her seat and began. 'You know why you're here, don't you, Sophie?'

'I guess.'

'You can't walk into a gym brandishing a rifle without getting arrested and questioned.'

Sophie shrugged.

'Actually, I want to take you back. Possession of a firearm with intent to endanger life can wait.' She sat up straighter. 'On the night Carmen Hope died – September – you got a message from Elizabeth Hope. Just after ten in the evening. You were near her house at the time. We checked your phone records. And you replied, before you turned your phone off. Can you explain why you were there?'

Remembering the duty solicitor's advice for handling tricky questions, Sophie replied, 'No comment.'

'Why did you turn your phone off at that point?

Sophie shrugged again. 'It was getting late. No one was going to call.' She tried to stop her brain summoning up a delicious image of Carmen Hope just after she'd smashed a heavy frying pan into the back of her head.

'You told your parents you were at home that night but that wasn't true, was it? We know it wasn't.'

'No comment.'

Zena glanced at the duty solicitor and smirked. 'We'll come back to it. I want to move on to the Florence Quinn case.'

Heavy lion ornament. Shiny forehead. Sound of

glass on skull like shoe cracking ice of frozen puddle. The joy of warm blood.

Sophie swallowed and refocused.

The detective asked, 'Am I right in thinking you'd been to the Quinns' house before Florence's untimely death?'

'Er … Sure.'

'Twice?'

'Yes.'

'And you went there … why?'

'Because Jonah's my friend.'

'Ah. Your running mate.'

Sophie nodded.

'And that's all he is?'

Sophie indulged in a slight smile. 'Yes.'

'Were you wearing your beanie hat on either of those occasions?'

'I don't know. I don't think so.'

'Are you sure?'

'Fairly sure. Why?'

The detective ignored her question. 'How did Jonah get on with his mum and dad?'

'Just to clarify,' the solicitor said, breaking into the exchange, 'I understand you've charged someone with the murder of Mrs Quinn.'

'Correct. Our enquiries continue.' To prompt an answer to her question, DI Kirkland raised her eyebrows even higher as she gazed across the table at Sophie.

'You can ask him. Jonah.'

'I want your opinion.'

'Like every kid, he grumbled about them.'

'All right. He's gay and they're homophobic. Does that sum it up?'

'I suppose.' Sophie hesitated before adding, 'But he didn't kill her. He was in London.'

It was the detective's turn to smile. 'I agree. It wasn't Jonah. Can you explain this, though? We found two fibres – the same as your beanie hat – attached to the wood of the utility cupboard – the one in the hall under the stairs. They were at head height.'

Sophie took a second to reply. 'Maybe I did wear it when I visited, then. It must have been where they put it.'

'You thought you didn't take it. You were pretty sure about that.'

'I made a mistake, I guess.'

'Mr Quinn doesn't remember you wearing a hat on either occasion.'

'He's wrong as well.'

'Neither does Jonah.'

'Look. I don't know. Maybe Jonah's got the same beanie,' said Sophie. 'Maybe the fibres are his.'

'We checked. He doesn't.'

Sophie looked at the duty solicitor. 'No comment.'

'It suggests to me you've been to the Quinns' house a third time. Wearing the hat.'

'No comment.'

'It suggests to me you hid in the under-stairs cupboard.'

Sophie shook her head.

'Do you remember the carpet in Mr and Mrs Quinn's bedroom?'

'Why should I?'

'Are you saying you didn't go into their bedroom?'

Another glance towards the only person who seemed to be on Sophie's side. 'No comment.'

'I'll remind you. The carpet had a really thick pile, freshly vacuumed. Ideal for retaining impressions of running shoes. Yours. You walked around and stopped by Mr Quinn's wardrobe, making quite a few shoeprints. Why was that?'

'No comment.'

DI Kirkland leaned forward. 'Were you putting on a few of his clothes?'

'No comment.'

'You're into forensic science, aren't you? You did work experience in it not that long ago.'

'Yes.'

'So you know all about blood spatter patterns.'

'A bit.' Sophie relished the wonderful spatter pattern she'd create if she walloped the detective's marbled forehead with her chair. She'd never feel that joy because the chair was fastened to the floor.

'Did you see the Quinns' alarm code on one of your previous visits?'

'No.'

DI Kirkland quoted the wrong number as she gazed carefully into her suspect's face.

Sophie tried not to react to the deliberate error. 'If you say so.'

'You should know I'm going to come back to these questions over and over again. It's a process of attrition and I'm going to do it till I get proper answers. For now, let's move on. Let's turn our attention to the garden wall that mysteriously collapsed.'

That triangular slab of stone. Thrusting, cracking, spurting.

Zena cocked her head on one side. 'Just for a moment there, Sophie, you seemed to be enjoying a memory. A look of pleasure came over your face.'

'Really? No.'

'Well, you couldn't have had anything to do with Denise Wilson's death because you were miles away in the shopping mall. Right?'

'I think so.'

'Your dad's got the evidence.'

'If you say so,' Sophie repeated.

'Except that you weren't. We've been through the CCTV very carefully indeed. You weren't there. But here's the thing. Your friend and lookalike, Ursula Graham, was. She stopped and sent a text – we've got it on camera – at exactly the time your Dad got a message from your mobile. Two minutes past three.' DI Kirkland's lips formed a warped smile. 'To give yourself an alibi, you did a phone swap with her, didn't you?'

'I don't know what you mean.'

'All right. I want to talk about some more impressions of your running shoes. They're very distinctive and they're all over the pathway beside Mrs Kelly's collapsed wall.'

'That's not a surprise. I've been running past her place a lot.'

'Mmm. But we've measured the distance between your shoeprints when you're running. You didn't just run past, did you? You stopped, walked up and down a bit.'

'Yeah. That's right,' Sophie admitted. 'Some boys had demolished part of the wall. I stopped to take a look.'

'It's quite a coincidence that Mrs Kelly got one of the Lady Gardener's business cards at the perfect time. You gave it to her, didn't you?'

Verity was a proper actress. Despite her name, she could lie like a professional. Sophie didn't believe she'd give the game away. 'No comment.'

'It's the strangest thing about that card. No fingerprints apart from Mrs Kelly's. Whoever gave it to her must have wiped it clean of prints. Who'd do that? And why?'

'You're the police officer, not me.'

'The stone that did the damage. It hit Mrs Wilson with a lot of force. It wasn't – couldn't have been – an accident. Someone was behind it. That was you.'

Sophie shook her head.

'We know it was you because there's a fibre on it that matches your running gloves.'

'When I stopped to look, I picked up one or two stones, I think.'

'Amazing coincidence that it happened to be the one that killed her. Anyway, you were miles away at the time. Except that we've talked to Ursula Graham … '

Sophie stiffened. Ursula wasn't like Verity. She would crack under pressure.

The senior investigating officer said, 'She told us all about the phone swap: what she got out of it, what you got her to do. She texted your father, bought some protein powder and gave you the receipt.'

'No comment.'

'I have to say, Sophie, it all looks very cold and calculated.'

Sophie did not reply.

'It's like a pack of cards, you know. When one card falls, the next one tends to as well. After talking to Ursula, we went back to Verity. She was very protective of you, but things have changed. Her mother's died. Everything's turned upside down for her. She told us you'd been asking a lot about her mum and she gave you one of her business cards. Have you still got it?'

'I don't think so. I don't know where it is. I wasn't interested. I ditched it, I suppose.'

'Let's have a look at your motive. I say "motive" –

not "motives" – because you only had one. Each time you killed, you were helping out a school friend, as you saw it. Elizabeth Hope, Jonah Quinn, Verity Wilson, Ursula Graham. All these friends grumbled to you about their parents – mostly their mothers – immediately before they died. Or nearly died, in the case of Emily Graham.'

'No comment.'

'Was it about helping them or was that an excuse to satisfy your craving for seeing mothers die? That's what this is all about, isn't it? It's what your brain thirsts after.'

'No comment.'

DI Kirkland sighed. 'You know, not so many years ago – when I was in the junior ranks – we all shed a tear for you, Sophie. Quite a few tears actually. Me included. And Sergeant Lightwing. We had Ben Clinkard in this same room for questioning – not that there was any doubt about what he'd done – when we realised what you'd been through. We had such sympathy for you. I'm truly sorry you're here now, but I don't have an option. It's my job to find out what happened.' She shuffled around in her seat. 'What do you feel when you see violence?'

'I don't see much. A playground scrap between boys and that's about it.'

'On telly or a film, then.'

'That's just acting.'

'Dr Nawaz showed you a video of someone hurting

themselves. She was perturbed by your reaction. No empathy, just amusement.'

'I don't remember.'

'How about when you shot three people?' Zena asked.

'No comment.'

'Oh, come on. We've talked to all three. That's one crime you can't deny. They all say it was you. For two of them, we've got a stack of witnesses as well. How did it make you feel? Powerful, scared, appalled? Or is it exciting, enjoyable and addictive?'

'No comment.'

'You know what I think?'

'No.'

'I think you had a choice. I think you could either live – unhappily – with the trauma of what your father did to your mother, or you could have it damped down by a new medical procedure. I don't know what you wanted but, because you were young, your new mum and dad – desperate to give you a better life – decided for you. They volunteered you for an experimental brain treatment. And it succeeded. The trouble is, it went too far. By attaching good thoughts to a bad memory, Professor Dench turned you into a murder junkie. Ranji Nawaz agrees with me. He made you yearn for what used to torment you. That's the truth of it, isn't it?'

'No comment.'

The duty solicitor said to Zena Kirkland, 'I want to

remind you that you're a police officer, not a trained psychiatrist.'

'I'm probing motive,' DI Kirkland snapped.

The responsible adult had been a silent bystander. The other four jumped when he spoke. 'It's time she had a break,' he muttered, nodding towards Sophie. 'She's a minor and this is an interview, not psychological warfare.'

DI Kirkland hesitated and then stood up. 'Okay.' She left her male colleague to announce the postponement of further questioning and turn off the recording.

33

Above the cell door, a tiny spider crawled haphazardly across the ceiling. Lying on the mattress, Sophie watched it for a while. It was an inoffensive little creature, lost in the vast desert of plain plaster. Not even the most ardent of arachnophobes would have been freaked out by this small moving speck. No need to call in Professor Dench and his amazing brain technology.

Sophie reflected on hours of questioning, hours of resisting, hours of not cracking. She reflected on saying, 'No comment,' a thousand times since her arrest. She also replayed DI Kirkland's last remark. 'The evidence has stacked up, Sophie. When it gets to a certain height, I put it to the Crown Prosecution Service and they make the next move. It's not up to me. We'll hold you here for at least twenty-four hours. In that time, the CPS will decide if you should be charged with anything and, if so, what.

Then … ' She'd hesitated and shrugged. 'One step at a time, eh.'

Sophie wondered whether and when she would take Jonah's advice and make the official announcement of her elevation to the role of serial killer. By strolling into the gym armed with a rifle, she had merely surrendered. That wasn't a confession. Threatening behaviour wasn't the same as admitting to murder. She was used to performing in front of a crowd. She wouldn't give DI Kirkland the pleasure of a confession, face-to-face in a small grey room with just a few police officers as an audience.

What, she wondered, was the collective noun for police officers? A proliferation of police officers? A gang? A posse? A line-up? She knew that when crows gathered together, it was called a murder of crows. Perhaps a collection of police officers could be called a crimewave. Eyes still following the lonely spider, she smiled to herself.

She imagined a triangle like the ones drawn by Dr Nawaz at the Institute for Memory Disorders, but different. One side represented motive. That drove Sophie to the second side: crime. Inevitably, that led to the third side which was all about punishment, justice and the law. That's where she was right now, waiting for the CPS's ruling.

The small crimewave of police officers included Zena Kirkland and her father. DI Kirkland looked uneasy and satisfied. Sergeant Lightwing looked perplexed and petrified.

'In a minute,' the senior investigating officer said, 'I'm going to read out the charges against you, Sophie. I have to do it formally and properly. But, before that, let me talk you through it. Okay? The CPS doesn't think we have the evidence to charge you with the murder of Carmen Hope. It's a different matter with Florence Quinn and Denise Wilson. You're going to be charged with murdering both of them.' A strangulated noise escaped from Sergeant Lightwing's throat, but DI Kirkland ignored it and got on with the task. 'Because of the incidents with Emily Graham and her rifle, you're going to be charged with assault, theft, and possession of a firearm with intent to endanger life. Because you fired the weapon at three people – including Jonah Quinn – there'll be charges of attempted murder as well. Anything else is trivial in comparison.' DI Kirkland looked into Sophie's face. 'Do you understand?'

'Yes.'

'Come on, then. Let's get it over with. Make it all official.'

34

Over the next weeks and months – it seemed like forever – Sophie was held on remand in a secure children's home. Various people were brought in to see her. She was taken to various others. She was sure they all meant well. They all seemed to have a job to do. Briefing her on the coming court case, psychiatric assessment, background checks, gauging her understanding of the charges against her. None of these people asked her about running. They wanted to tell her something about the legal process or review her mental state. She never knew that there were so many questions that began, 'How did you feel when … ?' The world was awash with them. When the experts eventually ran out of such questions, they started again at the beginning. 'How did you feel when you saw your biological dad … ?'

To Sophie, it seemed that she – as a whole person –

didn't exist any longer. All these people were interested in only one thing: the state of her brain.

'I see you're an exceptional runner,' Robert Munro said, glancing at some papers in his hand.

At once, Sophie came to attention. 'Seems like an age ago.'

'What's your PB?'

'Seventeen ten for 5k.'

'Wow. That's fast. I'm more of a tennis man myself, but I know that's serious running at your age.' He cast the papers aside. 'We'll see how quickly we can get you out of the legal system and back on the track.'

Robert didn't look like a tennis man. He was wrapped up in a smart suit and prim shirt with a crimson tie. Exactly what Sophie expected of a defence barrister.

'Let's get down to business,' he said, loosening his tie and undoing his top button. He propped his right leg on a stool and rested his left on top of it. 'Because of the seriousness of the charges, it'll go to Crown Court, not the Youth Court. But don't worry, they'll tone it down. Regular breaks, appropriate language, and they won't bother with wigs and full regalia.'

'Pity. I think men in wigs are funny.'

Robert looked across at Sophie and smiled slyly. 'Believe me, it's good news. You'll have a jury. We can play for their sympathy. Your background, your brain operation, even your running. A jury will lap it up. Take it into account.'

'Okay.'

'The prosecution's job is to persuade them you're guilty of murder. My job is to sow the seeds of doubt in their minds. If this were Wimbledon, we're starting at two sets down in a five-set match. The jury already thinks you're guilty because you're up in court. So, we've got to give them the opportunity to rethink their opinions. But two-nil isn't as bad as it sounds. Even if we started at nil-nil, we'd still have to win three sets. It's just that we can't make any slips. No wrong turns. There's one message I'm going to hammer over and over again – till the jury are hearing it in their sleep. If you hadn't had the brain treatment, you wouldn't have hurt anyone. Therefore, you're not to blame for anything. No matter what you've done or haven't done.'

Sophie nodded.

'You know when you put your foot in a pile of poo left on the pavement? Well, hardly anyone blames the dog. It's just doing what comes naturally. We always blame the owner, don't we? They didn't train the dog properly and they didn't clear up the mess either. It's much the same with your operation. Since that, you've just been doing what comes naturally. It's obvious the treatment wasn't carried out properly and whoever did it – this Professor Dench and his Ethics Committee – didn't clear up the mess afterwards. I'll make sure the jury buys the mad scientist stereotype. Again, not your fault.'

It seemed to Sophie that Robert Munro was as good at talking as she was at running. She hoped that his air of arrogance was born of experience and skill. No sign of a sense of humour, but he had bluntness by the bucketful. She liked him straightway.

'Do you drink coffee? We're both going to need it to get through this next bit.'

'I prefer something cold, loaded with sugar.'

Robert called for the drinks and switched his legs so the right rested on the left. 'I don't suppose you get to run here, do you?'

'Not really. No running track or anything. But I run round the building. With cameras and bouncers watching.'

Robert nodded. 'It must be frustrating.'

'Yeah.'

'Hang on in there.' He slapped his hand down on his case notes. 'I've been making various assumptions – well-grounded assumptions – about the way your trial's going to go. Now's the time to nail it down. You see, soon you're going to be arraigned. That means you're going to have to plead to the indictment, "guilty" or "not guilty" to everything on the charge sheet. In my opinion, it's hard to see anything but a guilty plea to some of the lesser charges like assault and theft of a firearm. They're incontestable. But let's start at the top. Murder.'

Robert hesitated while the drinks arrived. He started on the coffee immediately, even though it must have been very hot. He looked at Sophie and said, 'I've thought about you a lot. I reckon I've figured you out. Let me put it this way. If you're looking for a platform to unburden yourself, arraignment is it. It's your moment to look everybody in the eye and say, "Not guilty." Or you could stand there and admit it all. "Guilty." But there's a third option. You could say, "Not guilty to murder, but guilty to manslaughter by diminished responsibility." Let me explain.'

He took another drink of coffee. 'Manslaughter's not as serious as murder. In your case, it means you intended to kill but you had an abnormality of mind at the time. In other words, you were mentally ill. That's what diminishes your responsibility for the crime. Your illness was to blame. Are you with me?'

'Yes.'

'Before I go through the advantages and disadvantages of the various pleas, what are your thoughts? Do you need time to think about it or do you know what you want to do?'

'If you're going to defend me, don't you have to believe I'm innocent?'

'Not at all. I've defended some real nasty characters. I've spoken for people who've done the most unspeakable things. It's about doing the best for a defendant, that's all.'

'In that case … ' Sophie sighed. 'I might be ready to tell all.'

The barrister put his head on one side. 'What does that mean? In my profession, we use words very precisely – and carefully – to achieve the right effect. You need to help me do my job of helping you.'

'I'll tell everyone I'm guilty.'

'Of?'

'What you said. Manslaughter.'

'Guilty to manslaughter by diminished responsibility?'

'Yes, that.'

'Sure?'

'Yes.'

Robert nodded approvingly. 'I think that's best.'

'What does it mean?' Sophie asked.

'In terms of what'll happen?'

'Yes.'

'It means the main battleground's clear. The prosecution will try to convince the jury there's nothing wrong with you. No diminished responsibility. You're just a nasty piece of work who has murdered mums in cold blood. I'll trump them with medical evidence to the contrary,' he said confidently, removing his legs from the stool. 'You'll still be tried on two counts of murder and the other charges. If the jury agrees with the prosecution and finds you guilty of murder, you'll go to prison. If they agree with me and find you not guilty of murder, you'll avoid prison. You'll be convicted of manslaughter instead and you'll be given hospital orders. In other words, the diminished responsibility will mean you'll go to a secure hospital.'

'For how long?'

'There'll be no time limit,' Robert replied. 'Until you're deemed safe to release.'

Safe to release. She liked the sound of that. Safe to run again without her father's colleagues chasing her. But no further thrills beyond the finish line? It also seemed like torture. Cruelty. An unattainable state.

'We're getting ahead of ourselves,' Robert said, interrupting her thoughts. 'Let's get back to the trial. If you're wondering, I wouldn't dream of putting you on the stand to face the prosecution's questions. Or to tell all, as you put it. You can incriminate yourself all too easily when up against a professional. We'll let experts and witnesses tell their stories, rather than you.'

'Okay,' Sophie replied. 'Whatever you say.'

'We're going to have to talk a lot more before the proceedings get underway. I need to know exactly what you did and why, if I'm going to deliver the best possible outcome. I need to understand what was going on up here.' Robert tapped the side of his head. 'But not right now. We've both begun to clear the air. Let's call it a day at that. Give ourselves some quality thinking time.'

35

'Can you tell the court about yourself – professionally – and in what capacity you know the defendant?'

'I'm Dr Ranji Nawaz, head of the Institute for Memory Disorders, and for four years – from the age of nine – Sophie was my patient.'

'So it's fair to say,' the prosecution barrister replied, 'that you know Miss Lightwing very well indeed.'

'Yes.'

'Would you even describe her as a friend?' she asked.

'I like to think so, yes.'

'And you're qualified to the highest level in ailments of the human brain.'

'Yes. Specialising in memory issues.'

'Would you outline for us what the defendant's memory issue was when she was your patient?'

'Put simply,' Ranji said in a quiet but authoritative

voice, 'Sophie was brutalised – mentally, not physically – by seeing her mother suffer years of domestic abuse. In particular, the trauma that Sophie suffered as an eight-year-old by seeing her father attack and murder her mother made her withdraw from effective participation in the real world. She was not a fully functioning girl.'

'Bearing in mind that we are a lay audience, please tell us about the various treatments you tried on Miss Lightwing.'

Ranji went through the whole, frustrating series of talking therapies.

'And am I right in thinking that none of this produced the hoped-for effect? Miss Lightwing still could not lead a normal life?'

'That's right. There was no significant improvement.'

'Tell me what happened next.'

'This is when Professor Dench at the university came on the scene. He was looking for patients to join his research programme into treating trauma and phobias by a physical intervention.'

'The court will hear from Professor Dench later, but can you give your understanding of his physical intervention, as you put it?'

Briefly, Ranji explained Professor Dench's proposal.

'So, your patient would go to Professor Dench, receive his treatment and be cured? She would have a sound state of mind.'

'Yes. That was the plan.'

'As I understand it, Dr Nawaz, you were – shall we say? – unenthusiastic about this new form of brain treatment. Is that right?'

'Yes. I told Sophie's parents about it but I was careful not to recommend it.'

'Why not?'

'Because the human brain is complicated. Physical intervention can have unintended consequences.'

'Mmm. Unintended consequences.' The barrister hesitated for effect. 'What – in your expert opinion – were they?'

'Sophie's extreme fear of violence to mothers was over-corrected during the treatment. Her feelings were not just damped down. The pendulum swung too far the other way and it's clear she began to enjoy it.'

'Did you test that opinion?'

'Yes.' Ranji told the court about Sophie's unsettling reaction to her video of the treadmill accident.

'So, you find it all too easy to believe that Miss Lightwing could commit much the same crime as her father before her?'

'Sadly, yes.'

'Now, we'll hear from others that this killing spree was not Miss Lightwing's fault. She has diminished responsibility, the defence will argue, because she had a mental incapacity at the time of the killings. What do you think of that?'

'I don't think I'm qualified to judge. But I'm sure she

feels pleasure when she kills. Her brain has been modified to feel a reward when she attacks mothers.'

The barrister smiled. 'We can all feel a reward when doing something we shouldn't. We can get a buzz from mischief. It doesn't mean we have to do it.'

Ranji paused for thought. 'You could equate what drives Sophie with what drives a drug addict. It's a compulsion. She's a victim of her brain chemistry.'

'We're all aware of addiction. We're all inclined to blame the drug supplier rather than the addict. Indeed, the law tries its best to convict the supplier, but it doesn't turn a blind eye to the addict who feeds his or her addiction by committing crime. Sophie went to great lengths to cover up what she did. As we've already heard from the police and forensic experts, she was very devious about it. She sought to blame Mr Quinn for the murder of Mrs Quinn and made Mrs Wilson's fate look like an accident. That means she knew that what she was doing was wrong.'

'Actually, I disagree with that. Some of it, anyway. I don't think framing Mr Quinn was her way of covering up what she'd done. She thought he deserved punishment along with his wife, so she tried to get him a prison sentence. In other words, he was another victim. A case of her killing two birds with one stone.'

'I think most people – including the jury – would conclude that it takes a very sound mind to devise and carry out such a sophisticated scheme. In any event, the defendant took great care to avoid leaving evidence. And she went to considerable lengths to make Mrs Wilson's murder look accidental. This means that she knew perfectly well that her actions were wrong. She could have resisted the urge to kill. Let me ask this: is she sane?'

'In the sense that she acts rationally, yes.'

To stop Ranji expanding on her answer, the barrister said, 'Thank you. That'll be all.'

Ranji steeled herself as the defence barrister got slowly to his feet.

Robert Munro took his time. He adjusted his jacket, glanced around the courtroom and rearranged his notes before fixing his gaze on the witness. 'I'm interested in your diagnosis of Sophie's current state of mind. This metaphor of the pendulum swinging too far. She began to enjoy violence towards mothers, you said. Correct?'

'That's right.'

'How are you able to make such a diagnosis when Sophie hasn't been your patient since Professor Dench's treatment? You offered the court a diagnosis of her frame of mind when you've hardly seen her.'

'I did see her … '

'Informally?'

'Yes. At the end of a run in the park.'

'Ah. Yes. In a field while she was still recovering from a gruelling five-kilometre race. You showed her a few seconds of a video clip. I took a look at it as well. I thought it was funny. I laughed. Does that make me a multiple murderer?'

'No.'

'We'll show it to the jurors. If they giggle over the woman's mishap, are they murderers too?'

'Of course not. It's about Sophie's immediate reaction to the accident. Along with her altered behaviour.'

'Her behaviour? Are you prejudging Sophie before the jury has even had time to consider its verdict?'

'I meant, the Sophie I knew would not wander around with a rifle.'

'That happened well after your one-and-only flimsy test conducted while Sophie recovered from a long race.' Robert's eyes shifted towards the jurors. 'The members of the jury will be able to decide for themselves whether your examination was sufficiently thorough.' He changed tack. '"The Sophie I knew would not wander around with a rifle." Are you saying that Professor Dench's brain treatment was the cause of Sophie's change of direction?'

'Yes. Exactly.'

'Without that new and unproven procedure, she would not be here on these charges?'

'Certainly not.'

'So, let's be clear, her abnormal state of mind at the time of the crimes was the result of her brain operation? It was nothing to do with Sophie herself?'

'That's my opinion, yes.'

'What exactly were your concerns about Professor Dench's experimental method in Sophie's case?'

Ranji cleared her throat. 'Think about what makes any of us what we are. Our experiences. And not just the positive things in life like falling in love, having a once-in-a-lifetime holiday. Our negative experiences – a painful event, fear, a death in the family – shape us as well. Damp down the negative ones and we become different.'

'So,' Robert concluded, 'your reservations weren't specifically about the treatment going too far and causing a patient to enjoy – even become addicted to – a practice they once feared?'

'Not directly, no.'

'Interesting. This makes me wonder when you first believed that Sophie's treatment had gone wrong. That the pendulum had swung too far the other way.'

'The possibility arose when Detective Inspector Kirkland came to see me.'

'Let me get this straight. It only occurred to you – a brain expert – when DI Kirkland – a police officer, not a brain expert – talked about her suspicions. You didn't predict the problem.'

'With hindsight, or with criminal evidence, it seems rather obvious but, no, at the outset I didn't realise a brain would react like that to Professor Dench's procedure. I expected Sophie's memory of murder to be eased, not turned into a pleasure.'

'So, this side-effect was unforeseen by an expert,' said Robert.

'Yes.'

'Referring to Sophie's behaviour, you likened it to an addict seeking drugs. "It's a compulsion," you said.'

'Yes.'

'I just want to remind the jury of the definition of compulsion.' Robert turned to his computer screen and read aloud, "An irresistible urge to perform an act." He glanced around the courtroom. 'Irresistible. She had no choice.' He paused again. 'I suggest there's an alternative explanation for the lack of incriminating evidence against the defendant. The prosecution has it that Sophie covered everything up because she knew what she was doing was wrong. I don't think it's that at all. Does it make sense to you that her compulsion was so great that she avoided leaving clues simply so she could carry on seeking her highs?'

'That's perfectly reasonable.'

'So, she might not have thought she was doing wrong. In avoiding arrest, she was simply making sure she was free to follow what her altered brain compelled her to do.' Robert paused and repeated, '*Compelled* her to do.'

'It's possible, yes.'

'Thank you, Dr Nawaz.'

Robert adjusted his clothing yet again. 'Professor Dench. You heard how Dr Nawaz summed up your experimental brain procedure. Are you in agreement with what she said? Was it a fair summary?'

'Yes.'

'Good.' He waited for a moment before asking, 'Would you call yourself a responsible scientist?'

'Yes.'

'And a responsible father?'

The professor looked puzzled, but answered, 'Of course.'

'Mmm. You have a son, don't you?'

'Owen.'

'Yes. Owen Dench. He had a severe phobia of buttons, didn't he?'

Two jurors stirred, as if suppressing giggles.

'Yes. It's called koumpounophobia and it's particularly disabling. He couldn't wear most clothes, certainly not school uniform. He couldn't go to school. When he saw a button, he described it as like drowning, being unable to breathe.'

'Before Sophie Lightwing came along, you treated him in the same way, didn't you? You damped down his phobia, associating it with reward rather than fear.'

'Yes.'

'And how did that turn out?'

'Very well. He has a normal life now. He goes to school – in uniform.'

'So, your experiment on your son went well. That's a relief for all concerned. The fact that you did it in the first place might suggest to the jury that you were confident your technique was safe and successful, but there's another way of looking at it, isn't there?'

'Is there?'

'Some might think you're so driven as a scientist to promote your as yet unproven method that you used your own son as a guinea pig.'

'That's twisting it. Like any father, I just want what's best for him. I was confident I could help him, so I did – and it worked.'

'There are two ways of interpreting the word "responsible". You're also responsible for the outcome of this brain treatment.'

'Inasmuch as any medic is responsible for the outcome. All we can do is try our hardest for every patient.'

'I understand that your son – far from fearing buttons – now collects them as a hobby.'

'He does, yes.'

'And another person in your trial with an extreme fear of spiders – after the same procedure – keeps them as pets.'

'Yes.'

'And someone with acrophobia – fear of heights – turned into a rock climber.'

'Yes.'

'So, people who feared spiders, heights and buttons became obsessive about them – *loved* them, you might say – and it didn't occur to you that a patient who feared violence might start regarding it as enjoyable, obsessive, even compulsive?'

'If I'd been aware of that possibility, I would have discussed it with the patient and her parents first.'

'Neither you nor Dr Nawaz predicted a problem with your method. You just went ahead?'

'Violence is different from spiders, heights and buttons. I would have assumed that the moral imperative – the instinct we all have for doing the right thing – would have taken precedence and stopped any wrong-doing.'

'But it didn't.'

'I can assure you that all my work is overseen – and approved – by the Ethics Committee.'

'So, you're passing the blame for the consequences to a higher authority?'

'I'm simply telling you that all necessary permissions were in place and no one expected an adverse outcome.'

'Well, now you and your Ethics Committee have the benefit of hindsight,' said Robert. 'Are you still offering this brain procedure?'

'No.'

'So, you're admitting there's a problem with it.'

'We intend to review the situation after this trial.'

'Do you agree that Sophie has been left with an abnormal state of mind, that she could be likened to an addict, compelled to commit acts of violence as a habit?'

Professor Dench sighed heavily before replying. 'All the evidence suggests that is the case.'

36

Sophie's mind drifted away from the cut and thrust of examination and cross-examination. She gazed at the judge instead. She was sitting there, aloof, overseeing the proceedings, saying little, listening intently, reminding the defence barrister that the defendant was on trial, not a scientific method and not its inventor. Every now and then, she interceded with a decision or instruction from on high. She was like a goddess about to raise her hands and pass judgement on the petty humans beneath her. But Sophie wasn't fooled. She knew where the real power lay and it wasn't with the judge. The jury – randomly selected members of the public – would make the crucial decisions.

The middle-aged man at the end of the first line of jurors was bored. His eyes told Sophie that his attention lay elsewhere. There were a hundred other places he'd prefer to be and a hundred important things he needed to do. The fifty-something woman next to him was the opposite. Fully engaged, determined to do her bit for society. But she had a pinched, harsh face. She would easily mutter, 'Guilty.'

The next member of the jury was a young man. Quite cool, actually. And hot. He looked suitably serious and sympathetic. Occasionally, he glanced at Sophie, never critically, trying to understand. Probably trying to think of a way she could be helped rather than punished.

The fourth juror was either putting on a little weight around the waist or, more likely, she was pregnant. A mother-to-be. Maybe already a mother. She seemed endlessly surprised and horrified by the threat that Sophie posed to her kind. Juror number five wore a thin sports shirt. He was probably in his thirties and he was far too muscular to be a distance runner. Thick neck, wide chest, arms like tree trunks. Perhaps a sprinter. He was certainly into weight-lifting. Sophie assumed that Robert would have noted the gear he wore every day and would mention her athletic credentials at some point to play for his vote.

At the far end of the first row there was a retired man in a jacket and tie. Very formal, he took his civic duty earnestly, but he also wore an indecisive expression most of the time. He seemed to be waiting for the one solid fact that, above all others, would allow him to come to the right verdict.

Sophie's trial had thrown together twelve assorted people who would never normally sit together. Afterwards, they'd scatter and probably never meet again. Once they'd gone through the motions and declared the result of their deliberations, they might not even think of Sophie ever again.

Robert Munro called on a witness he named as Mrs Johnson. 'I'd like you to tell the court about your first encounter with Sophie Lightwing, the defendant.'

The weekend warrior described tripping during a run and gashing her head. She described how Sophie and her male friend, also out on a run, slowed and stopped. 'She was a smashing girl, as far as I could make out. She asked me if I was all right but realised I needed help. She turned her friend's top into a bandage, stopped the bleeding with it and walked me back to the medical room.'

'And later you saw her for a second time, under what circumstances?'

'In the gym, threatening everyone with a rifle.'

Robert nodded. 'Did you say anything to her?'

'I asked if she remembered me.'

'And did she?'

'Yes. Actually, she was a bit strange. She said, "You bashed your head. It was great." Or words to that effect.'

'As if she enjoyed head injuries?'

'Exactly.'

'What went through your mind at the time?'

'I didn't understand how such a nice girl could wave a gun around like that all of a sudden. It seemed way out of character to me.'

'Then what happened?'

'She shot me.'

'Do you know why?'

'I suppose because I didn't go where she told me to go. Not straightaway.'

'Did she aim at your heart or your head?'

'No. I think it was a warning shot. I have a little scar on my shoulder. No more than that.'

'So, you're a victim, but you're saying Sophie wasn't attempting murder?'

'I don't think so, no.'

'We'll hear later that her best friend had advised her to give herself up to the police. Could it be that she had no intention of endangering life at all with that rifle? Could it be that she was simply announcing herself to the police – and the world? A showy sort of surrender.'

'She could have sprayed the place with bullets but she didn't, so it's more than likely,' Mrs Johnson replied.

When Jonah Quinn came to the witness box and promised to tell the whole truth, Sophie felt comforted to have him with her in the courtroom. She knew that, under examination, he'd make her look guilty, but he was still a friendly young face in a sea of adult hostility.

He answered all of the prosecution's questions briefly. He stuck resolutely to the bare facts and offered nothing else. Even when the barrister gave him the opportunity to condemn her, he refused it.

'Do you blame Sophie Lightwing for your mother's death?'

'No,' Jonah replied. 'I blame something wrong in her head.'

Sophie liked to think his responses were measured so he didn't dig a deeper hole for his running mate. He loosened up only when Robert Munro began his cross-examination.

'How did you meet Sophie?' Robert asked.

'At a race. A five-kilometre run.'

'Ah, yes. You're both very good runners.'

'I'm all right, but Sophie's something else. She's going to be world class.'

Robert nodded and smiled in the direction of the jury. 'Yes. She's very talented, I'm told.'

'You ought to see her. She glides like no one else.'

'Did you become friends?'

'Yes. We trained together.'

'Is that all?'

'We hung out, yes.'

'How would you describe her?'

'Friendly, funny, kind … '

‘Kind.’ Robert nodded. ‘And is she still a friend?’

Jonah glanced at Sophie. ‘I think so.’

Robert drew in a breath, puffing himself up. ‘It’s quite something for you to choose to remain friends with someone accused of your mother’s murder.’

‘I’m sure she did it, but she thought she was doing me a favour because I didn’t get on with my mum and dad. Anyway, it wasn’t really her. It’s like something wrong in her brain made her do it.’

‘“Something wrong in her brain made her do it,”’ Robert repeated, to ram the point home to the jury. ‘Would you say that diminished her responsibility?’

‘Totally.’

‘And when you realised what she’d done, what did you do?’

‘I told her to give herself up.’

‘This was just before the incident in the gym with the rifle?’

‘Yes.’

‘So, were the people in the gym really under threat or was she just giving herself up to the police – in an elaborate way?’

‘I think it was all for show.’

‘She shot you, though.’

‘That was just a tussle for the gun. I tried to take it off her.’

‘Are you saying it was an accident?’

‘Yes.’

'Not attempted murder?'

'No way.'

'The fact that you still describe her as a friend tells us you don't believe there was malicious intent on her part.'

'That's right.'

Questions came and went. Countless experts and witnesses came and went. Verity Wilson, Ursula Graham, Emily Graham, Mrs Kelly, Sophie's parents, Peter Quinn, a couple of teachers. Even Mike, the forensic scientist. Some painted Sophie in a good light, others didn't. Sometimes, Sophie felt she was about to be found innocent of everything. She was ready to reach for her running shoes. Other times, she feared the worst. She could almost hear the prison doors slamming shut. And still the trial continued. Day after day. An endless supply of talking heads. The process seemed set to carry on forever.

Sophie wondered if the jury experienced the same ups and downs. At one key moment, they were perhaps itching to acquit. At the next, they probably wanted to throw the key away. And they probably wanted the process to end as well.

The back row of jurors was as diverse as the front. Sophie guessed that, taken together, they were supposed to represent the country's makeup. They had the required spectrum of skin colour and ethnicity. If one were transgender, another disabled and one gay, they'd probably have it all covered. If clothing reflected wealth and class, again there was a spread. If one was a genius, another stupid and the rest in between, she had no way of knowing. Skinny, obese, young, old, short, tall, weak, strong, hairy and bald: the jury had it all.

The nearest man in the second line – the seventh juror – repeatedly polished his glasses on a handkerchief. His stubble was a curious mixture of grey and black. He looked depressed most of the time, with a *what's-the-world-coming-to?* expression on his face. Occasionally, he looked upwards as if seeking divine guidance. Sophie guessed that he was religious.

The eighth member of the jury – a younger man – had paid particular attention to Jonah's testimony. He seemed impressed by the bond between witness and defendant. Impressed that it had outstripped crime.

The last four members of the jury were all female. Number nine was definitely not a runner. She was old and haggard and walked with a stick, but once, perhaps, she might have been imposing and gracious. Worn but warm. Maybe she was the genius of the bunch. Next to her was an overweight twenty-something. Her hair was pulled back severely from her face and tied very tightly behind her head. Her pale scalp showed through. It looked painful. Sophie wondered why she didn't go for short hair instead. Her earrings were enormous and dangled onto her shoulders. She chewed constantly and hardly reacted to the twists and turns and new revelations.

Number eleven looked at Sophie regularly, mostly with disdain. This juror was not going to be swayed by descriptions of Sophie as friendly and kind. She was not going to be swayed by athletic promise. Sophie even doubted if she would be swayed by the notion of a mental abnormality. The final one – juror twelve – was a good listener. She was also the sort of woman who mesmerised men. Sophie could imagine the boys at school drooling over her and making lewd comments. The last juror was definitely one reason why the first was so distracted. But Sophie saw something behind the face and the figure. She envisaged a confident, perceptive and persuasive juror. This woman looked like she could handle unwanted attention and a wayward bunch of opinions.

Sophie felt she knew each of the people who were her real judges – as much as she could know anyone from a distance across a room. She hadn't exchanged a single word with any of them. She had only their body language and expressions to decode. Before they retired into a huddle to begin their discussions, though, Sophie guessed they were split in their views of her culpability. Would they ever be unanimous, and which way would they go? She didn't really have a clue.

Opposite the jury, Sophie's parents sat nervously in the gallery. Clearly, they didn't know where to focus. Their eyes flitted in turn from Sophie, to a witness, the barristers, the judge and the jury. They too were looking for small signs of support or disapproval.

Sophie felt totally out of control. This large complicated machine called the justice system had consumed her. When it had finally finished chewing, it would spit her out. She didn't know where or in what state.

37

Before the jurors left to consider their verdicts, they had to listen to the closing addresses of the case. Juror number one was already beyond boredom and frustration. Eyeing number twelve was his only compensation. The sixth member of the jury nodded thoughtfully as the prosecution barrister highlighted her key points, damning Sophie. At exactly the same moments, juror eight shook his head in disagreement.

'Let's not judge this particular book by its cover,' said the barrister, wheeling out the tired cliché straightaway. 'The fact is, inside an attractive exterior, there's a brutal, perverted, blood-thirsty story. It doesn't matter whether its author – the person responsible for the carnage – is an Olympic prospect. It doesn't matter how kind someone says Sophie Lightwing is. You're here to consider only what she's done. And we have all heard the extreme levels of her plotting, worthy of any crime novel. She did not just kill two mothers and threaten to kill many more. It was the way she did it that's so galling. No remorse, no empathy, utterly devious, avoiding detection, blaming someone else. Miss Lightwing is wicked and sly, a monstrous schemer. And that level of cleverness and planning is proof that her mind is fully functioning. Indeed, her own brain specialist assures us that she is rational and perfectly sane. I contend that the defendant was of sound mind at the time of the murders.

'Here's just one example. She's already admitted the manslaughter of Denise Wilson, but it wasn't like any manslaughter I know. It was highly calculated. First, she got her father to find her work experience in Vehicle Forensics. Why? Because Mrs Wilson drove the school bus. Miss Lightwing even asked her supervisor about tampering with brakes. I think we all know what was going through her mind. Could she kill poor Denise Wilson by sabotaging the bus she was driving? The answer was straightforward. With modern safety features, it would be extremely difficult so she abandoned that idea and turned to Mrs Wilson's other occupation as gardener. This provided the defendant with an easier option for carrying out her warped plan to murder.'

Sophie turned off while the prosecution barrister continued to let rip, splattering her canvas with vivid jarring colours like Edvard Munch painting *The Scream*. Her description of Sophie was so alien – as if she were talking about some other girl entirely. In her head, Sophie formed her own silent scream.

Eventually, it was Robert Munro's turn to captivate and convince the jury. 'We're not denying that Sophie here went off the rails. She did. But it's essential to ask yourselves why. Sophie didn't *choose* to derail. She didn't intend to be that way. That wasn't Sophie at all. And it wasn't a form of malice. Given that it was way out of character, you have to ask yourselves what caused her recent behaviour. Because that's what's to blame, not Sophie.

'As we've heard, Sophie was a vulnerable, meek and very likeable girl. Going boldly into the world was not what she was about.' He paused as if he was considering something that had just come to his mind. 'Can you imagine what it's like to experience the extreme level of domestic violence that an eight-year-old Sophie saw? Can you imagine the effect it'd have? No. Sophie withdrew from the world. She was shy and retiring. Tragic. She wasn't the convenient, fictional monster the prosecution's summoned up to influence your thinking.'

Robert shook his head sadly as if he believed there was an Oscar up for grabs. 'It was Sophie's brain operation that knocked her off course. We all know it, don't we? That's what did it. Now, I'm sure Professor Dench was acting with the best of intentions and his experiments were approved by an Ethics Committee. But all these clever people were glaringly naive.' He pronounced 'clever' as if it were an insult. 'They failed to predict an obvious side-effect. The unproven procedure certainly removed the trauma of maternal death and instead made Sophie feel great about it. But we're not here to judge Professor Dench and what happened at the university. We're here to think about Sophie.' He wound up the emotion in his voice. 'You can't blame – or punish – anyone for trying a new medical treatment to fix their health. What happened was ... ' He shrugged. 'Bad luck. That's all. She was cured and corrupted. From that point, Sophie had no choice in the matter. Her altered brain ruled her behaviour. She was turned into an addict. She was compelled to act. To quote Dr Nawaz – the expert who knows her best – "It's a compulsion. She's a victim of her brain chemistry. " She's a victim! Yes. A victim of a treatment that went wrong. And in a court of law we should not be putting victims on trial.'

That was just the starter. He also served up a main course, landing blow after blow on the prosecution's case, ramming home his message time and again that an abnormal state of mind meant diminished responsibility and ruled out murder, mesmerising the jurors with his performance, his passion. By the time he'd finished, he had made it clear that only a bunch of heartless brutes could convict her of anything more serious than dropping litter. Robert sat down and the trial was almost complete.

Like a pompous headteacher, the judge gave the jury instructions: what they must do and how to do it. She reminded them that they might find Sophie Lightwing guilty of murder but, if they acquitted her of the most serious counts, she would still be guilty of the lesser contained offence of manslaughter because that is how she had pleaded.

And with that, Sophie's exam was over. Pens down. Nothing more could be added and nothing noted could be subtracted. Only the marking and the announcement of results remained to be done. The members of the jury filed out of the courtroom in apprehensive silence.

#1. 'Let's convict the kid and get it over with, so we can get on with our own lives.'

#2. 'If you ask me, she's inherited a violent streak from her real father. Simple as that. Dangerous DNA.'

#3. 'I'm sure she's guilty of everything – and more. But I'm even more sure she's not to blame. If she hadn't had the brain treatment, she wouldn't have been like she is. She wouldn't have hurt a fly. It's not her fault.'

#4. 'I'm a mother. I wouldn't feel safe with her around. She might be innocent – in the sense that it wasn't her fault – but the public's still got to be protected from her. She's got to be put away.'

#5. 'You might as well blame her adoptive parents. They were desperate to give her self-confidence. She's not responsible. Her brain made her do it.'

#6. 'I don't buy it. There's always choice. We can all apply the brakes to our … crazy impulses. We can refuse pleasure if we're so minded. This girl chose not to.'

#7. 'She is one of God's children. Imperfect like the rest of us, but not evil. In her case, science let her down, perverted her from the straight and narrow. The blame? That lies with those who think science provides the answer to everything. It doesn't.'

#8. 'The boy – Jonah Quinn – stuck by her. Even after his mum died. That says it all to me. If he can see the good in her, we should as well.'

#9. 'I feel so sad. Such a waste. Slapping a label of murderer on her won't help put things right. Neither will locking her up. Prison will do more harm than good. We have to give a verdict that will allow her some treatment – to try and repair what's been done. To turn her back into a useful member of society.'

#10. 'She's weird but she was only looking after her friends, getting rid of stupid parents like her brain told her. That's never murder. Not in my mind.'

#11. 'Pity we didn't hear what the girl had to say for herself, but she's guilty as sin.'

#12. 'It's not black and white, is it? Not a simple yes or no. Personally, I don't think murder's the right word for what she did, but we've all got our different opinions. I think we need to start at the top – the murder charge – and work our way down, deciding where her culpability kicks in.'

38

By the time Sophie saw the jury again, days later when they shuffled back into the courtroom as awkwardly as they'd left it, juror twelve had transformed into a spokesperson. She told the judge that there was no chance that they would come to unanimous verdicts on the major charges. Not even if they batted the arguments back and forth for a month.

The judge sent them out again to try to come to majority decisions instead.

#1. 'For the sake of getting this thing over with, I can live without a murder charge.'

#2. 'All right. She's far from innocent but, if we're sure everyone will still be protected from her, count me in.'

#3. 'That defence barrister was pretty convincing. She's definitely not to blame. I'm onside.'

#4. 'Ditto.'

#5. 'It's the best compromise we've got.'

#6. 'No. I disagree. She chose to kill. She committed murder. I'm not in, onside or anything else. I'm deeply unhappy.'

#7. 'It's not in our power to blame those who are responsible. We're only human and it's the best we can do. God will judge everyone – including us – long after this day's done.'

#8. 'I'm sticking with my decision. If Jonah Quinn stays on her side, so do I.'

#9. 'She's already pleaded guilty to manslaughter. Turning it into murder isn't fair. This way, we've been told she'll end up in a secure hospital. Let's hope they can put things right.'

#10. 'Yeah. I never thought it was proper murder.'

#11. 'Too many of you are just going with the flow. She's guilty of everything. It's obvious.'

#12. 'Okay. We're not all in agreement – and that's the way it's going to stay, I think – but shall I say we've done all we can and we've got verdicts?'

The next day, the judge asked the foreperson, 'Have you reached verdicts on which at least ten of you agree?'

'We have. Yes.'

Robert sat up straight, telling Sophie that her time had come. In the gallery, her parents tensed. This was it. Heaven or hell.

The murder of Denise Wilson. 'Not guilty.'

The murder of Florence Quinn. 'Not guilty.'

Attempted murder of Emily Graham. 'Guilty.'

Attempted murder of Anne Johnson. 'Not guilty.'

Attempted murder of Jonah Quinn. 'Not guilty.'

Possession of a firearm with intent to endanger life. 'Not guilty.'

To Sophie's ear, all those negatives sounded wonderful. Not guilty. Not responsible. Not her fault. Not heading for prison. But she wasn't going to walk away from the courtroom. She had tried to kill Ursula's mum. And she'd already pleaded guilty to the manslaughter of Denise Wilson and Florence Quinn, assault and the theft of a firearm. She had already announced herself. High voltage, Jonah would have said. Totally guilty of those charges. She would be sentenced. She would be given hospital orders. She would be packaged up and stored away safely, out of sight, out of reach.

39

Sophie knew it was no ordinary visit. Her parents looked nervous and they were accompanied by two people she hadn't seen for ages. 'We've had an idea,' Tony said. 'It's taken a lot of talking with the legal side of things as well as … ' He nodded towards the visitors.

Her mum took up the story. 'You see, nothing's going to get done – nothing's going to change – unless you're treated. We'll never give up. We've got to make you better if you're going to get out of here. We've come up with something that might well help, but you're over eighteen now. An adult. You've got to make the final decision.'

'What's the plan?' Sophie asked.

Her mum and dad both turned to look at Professor Dench.

'It's this,' he replied. 'I think there's a way of making

you better, of "correcting" your brain, if you like. I'd show you lots of images. They'd all be about motherhood, one way or another. Pictures of pregnant women and new mums with their babies. Your own mum, this mum,' the professor waved towards Grace Lightwing, 'will feature heavily. That sort of thing. I'd monitor your brain while you're looking. Then, when those same areas light up in sleep, I'd stimulate the reward centres of your brain.'

Sophie was silent for a few seconds. 'So, it's exactly what you did before, but different.'

'Yes. We're not damping down a trauma or anything like that. We're using the same technique to re-establish a humane view of mothers. We believe that will override the last treatment, eliminating your addiction to maternal violence.'

'And making me safe to release?'

'I hope so. This plan's got the blessing of the hospital, the Ethics Committee and the legal authorities.'

Clearly on edge, her mum said, 'You've got to tell her about possible side-effects. Like she might end up being ... withdrawn again.'

'That's got to be a risk,' Ranji Nawaz said. 'If you suddenly adore mothers, you might be devastated all over again by what happened to your biological mother.' She shrugged. 'We just don't know. We're in unchartered water here.'

'But,' Professor Dench added, 'you've got to ask

yourself if being bothered by trauma is any worse than how things are right now, being kept in a secure hospital because you're too dangerous to be in the community.'

'Have a few days to think about it, love,' her dad said.

Sophie smiled. 'I don't need days, minutes or anything else.' After years of stagnation, Sophie would clutch at anything. 'It's got to be worth a try to get me out of here. Show me the photos.'

40

When a reporter with a sly grin stood up, Andrea Pullman felt a sudden chill in the press interview. The respectful questions about her running, her 10km medal, were over. Dread gripped her. 'Congratulations. You looked terrific out there. My question is this. Is it true, Andrea, that before you were Andrea Pullman, you were Sophie Lightwing and, before that, Sophie Clinkard?'

Andrea sat there, mouth open, unable to say a word.

Her agent jumped up, positioning herself between Andrea and the reporter. 'That's enough! We're here to talk about her spectacular achievement. Nothing else.' She grabbed Andrea's arm and marched her out of the room.

But it was too late. Her anonymity had been breached. The pack of hounds had been released.

Outside, a driver leaned out of his car window and shouted, 'Andrea. Over here.'

A bodyguard stood between the car and the pursuing pack of hounds. No one was going to get past him.

Amazed and grateful, Andrea ran to the car and jumped into the passenger's seat.

'Taxi, ma'am? To take you somewhere safe.'

She looked around at the bodyguard. Like a dam wall, he was holding back the flood. 'But … '

The driver smiled. 'You once told me to date a bodyguard. He's a high-voltage good 'un. He'll catch up with us later.'

'But … '

'I wasn't going to miss your big race, was I? But I thought the press might turn ugly. It's not hard to trace who you are. So I came prepared. Left the engine running.'

'Okay.' After all these years, she trusted him completely. 'Let's go.'

Jonah's foot slammed down on the accelerator.

'Your name never got in the news. "For legal reasons, we can't name … " I think it was you being young,' Jonah said. 'But anyone at the gym that day, or the kids and mums at your school, they would've all known. It was only a matter of time before it got leaked to the press.'

Andrea sat on the sofa in Jonah's flat and sighed.

'I heard about this fantastic new distance runner and

I knew straightaway. I've been secretly stalking you.' Jonah handed her a cold sports drink. 'The police can't give you another new identity. Not unless you stop running and winning. You've just been on telly as Andrea Pullman. It'd look a bit weird if you turned up to your next race as someone no one's heard of.'

Andrea shook her head. 'It's like I'm still being punished. This time, it's the press who're having a go at me.'

'I don't think they're allowed to print anything about who you are. So maybe it's okay. Anyway, you can't stop running. Maybe you can carry on, but only talk to the BBC or others who are going to play fair.'

'I've got an agent. Maybe she can vet any interviews.'

'Sounds good to me.'

'She's probably sending a hitman round to that reporter right now.'

'Let's hope so.'

For the first time since that horrible question, Andrea smiled. She looked around the flat and said, 'So this is where you live now.'

Jonah nodded. 'With George the bouncer. We're thinking of getting married.'

'Will you invite me?'

'There'll be a place reserved for Andrea Pullman. Is that what we call you?'

'Yes.'

'You'll be there.'

'Don't set a date during the Olympics.'

'Good point.'

'What do you do now?' Andrea asked.

Jonah hesitated. 'I'm almost ashamed to tell you. I'm not in contact with my dad, but I am a doctor.'

'What?'

'I run for the county as well. Not as high-voltage as you, but … '

'Do you want to run with me again sometime?'

'I thought you'd never ask,' said Jonah. 'We might have to train George as well – so he can keep journalists off our backs.'

'He looked too beefed up to me.'

'Beefy and strong. He doesn't let the public see his cuddly side. He could follow us on a bike.'

'It's a deal.'

Jonah paused and then looked into his visitor's face. 'They let you out. That means you've had treatment. What happened?'

'Professor Dench.' Sticking to the story that bought her release, she said, 'Exactly the same way as before. He tweaked my brain. This time, it was to make me love mothers all over again.'

'And obviously it worked.'

'Yeah.'

'That's really good news.'

Considering Professor Dench was intelligent, it had been surprisingly easy to pull the wool over his eyes.

Andrea had feared going back into her shell. From there, she believed she'd never run competitively again. She couldn't live without that thrill. She couldn't live without other thrills, either. She didn't want to change. So she'd cheated. Sure, she'd gawped at the professor's pretty pictures but what was in her mind at the time was definitely not affection. Unknown to Professor Dench, he'd rewarded her brain for pretending.

She'd also pulled the wool over the eyes of several experts and panels. That was easy too. She refrained from murdering anyone during the assessments and she said all the right things about mothers. No problem to outsmart a lot of smart people.

'Are you okay?' she asked.

Instantly, Jonah knew she was referring to the shooting in the gym. Pointing to his ear and then his waist, he said, 'Two impressive scars. That's all.' He paused before adding, 'We've got a spare room if you want to stay tonight. Just in case the bad guys are camped outside your mum and dad's place.'

'Thanks. I'll text them and let them know.'

41

There was no encampment outside her house. It wasn't because the press had lost interest in Andrea Pullman's backstory. They had simply been warned off by the family lawyer, the UK Athletics legal team and the police.

'We found out who that rogue reporter was,' her dad said, 'and sent the lawyer round – to remind him about the law, your rights and what he's allowed to publish. In no uncertain terms.'

'Thanks.' Andrea glanced at her mother, unable to ignore her sudden frostiness. 'What's the problem?' she asked.

'You took off with a man you hardly know. You should've turned to us.'

'I think I know Jonah pretty well – even if it's been a while.'

'He could have … hidden motives,' said Grace. 'Because of his mother. You know.'

'He doesn't keep his motives hidden. If he had a problem with me, he'd say.'

'You even shot him once.'

'Twice,' Andrea replied.

Her mother shook her head and scowled. 'You can't be too careful.'

'He was the first to react to the press conference. That's all. He got me out of there quicker than anyone else.'

'Yes. And then you stayed overnight.' Grace glanced at the clock.

'I'm a big girl now, Mum. I can make my own decisions. I was lying low till it blew over.'

'Mmm.' Grace's expression suggested that she regretted her daughter had grown up.

'Don't make me wish I'd stayed there,' Andrea snapped.

'He won't have forgotten what happened to his mother.'

'He doesn't blame me,' Andrea replied. 'Like the jury and everyone else.'

'I think you should steer clear of him.'

'We're going out training together sometime.'

Her mum ran out of words and patience. She let out a brazen groan instead.

Andrea looked at her dad and then back at her mum.

'You've done so much for me over the years. I can't thank you enough. I can't possibly repay you. But I need my own space. Especially now. I need to make the most of my second chance. I'm hoping you'll carry on giving me help and support. I still need it.'

'I've got to go to work,' her mother replied, 'but we're not helping you open up old sores.'

Andrea got up and left.

She was running at 60 per cent capacity. Even so, Andrea glided effortlessly past three other runners and two older men on bikes. The path bent round to the right, past the waste and recycling depot where her mother would be doing whatever she did on the evening shift.

Andrea slowed and glanced around. By the light of the lamps dotted along the path, she saw no one. Instead of leaning into the bend, she ducked through a gap in the railings on her left and crossed the dark untidy track, dashing unseen into the car park where her mum's car stood. There were only three other cars. The factory lights blazed. The nearest door was closed. Trying the handle with her gloved fingers, she found it was also locked.

She shrank into the shadows when a waste lorry came round the corner of the building. It crawled across an access area and up to a huge automatic door that slid back, welcoming it to the interior. Seeing an opportunity,

Andrea sprinted to the door and slipped inside just before the aluminium doors closed. She found herself in a huge room as big as a football pitch. The lorry pulled up to a pile of smelly rubbish, tilted its back end and regurgitated junk.

Her mum was a supervisor. Andrea didn't expect her to be roaming around the mucky end of the business. Instead, she went up a metal staircase. She imagined anyone overseeing the processes would be up on high, a solitary spectator on the balcony above the factory floor. To Andrea's right, a massive sorting machine was separating paper, glass, metal and plastic, sending each off on a different conveyor belt. Below, a giant crusher was making bundles of trash like bales of hay. This was the vicious machine that had caused the grotesque accident, severing half of a careless worker's arm. Andrea gazed down at the metal claws ripping and compressing. She smiled. Flesh and bone would not stand a chance. Andrea could easily imagine her mum's fate. Falling head first into the same machine. Just think. It would be gross and glorious.

'Andrea!' her mum yelled above the din of the machines. 'What are you doing here?'

'I just wanted us to make up. I didn't want … you know.'

'You shouldn't be here. How did you get in?'

Andrea stayed directly above the crusher, forcing her mum to come closer, to exactly the right position. 'Easy.

I just walked in with that lorry.' She pointed to the vehicle that was now leaving. 'No one said anything.'

Grace put her hand on her daughter's shoulder. 'Look. It's great that you want us to settle our differences, but you'll get me shot if anyone knows you're here.'

This was the moment. Grab her mum's hand from off her own shoulder. Grip her lower down with her other hand. Lift her up onto the rail and over. Watch her plunge down head-first into the crusher. Easy. Then experience everything that Andrea desired. The crunching sound. The fountain of blood.

She felt the irresistible surge of endorphins and oxytocin. Indescribable pleasure. A high like no other.

Andrea stepped up to 75 per cent capacity as she drove herself into the bend. A woman shortened her dog lead to make sure that her pet didn't wander into Andrea's path. Andrea hardly noticed. She went up to 90 percent just for the hell of it. She was enjoying her ability to fly. She was relishing her ability to imagine. She was wallowing in her new-found ability to pretend.

For now, that was enough.

Malcolm Rose is an established, award-winning author, noted for his gripping crime/thriller stories – all with a solid scientific basis.

Before becoming a full-time writer, Malcolm was a university lecturer and researcher in chemistry.

He says that chemistry and writing are not so different. *'In one life, I mix chemicals, stew them for a while and observe the reaction. In the other, I mix characters, stir in a bit of conflict and, again, observe the outcome.'*